# OPEN HOUSE

A Mystery Novel by

## FRAN SILVER

Order this book online at www.trafford.com
or email orders@trafford.com

Most Trafford titles are also available at major online book retailers.

Printed in Victoria, BC, Canada.

ISBN: 978-1-4269-1727-1 (soft)
ISBN: 978-1-4269-1728-8 (hard)

Library of Congress Control Number: 2009937379

*Our mission is to efficiently provide the world's finest, most comprehensive book publishing
service, enabling every author to experience success. To find out how to publish your book, your
way, and have it available worldwide, visit us online at www.trafford.com*

*Trafford rev. 11/16/2009*

 www.trafford.com

**North America & international**
toll-free: 1 888 232 4444 (USA & Canada)
phone: 250 383 6864 ♦ fax: 812 355 4082

# Preface

The motel manager momentarily surveyed the young man up and down. "Passing through or here on business perhaps?"

The men remained motionless, but for his hand scribbling over the credit card slip.

Raising his head for an eye to eye, "I suppose you could say that. Spent some time looking at property for sale around, Smithson County, I believe it's called? Sound right"?

"That's it, complied the manager, studying the credit receipt through the smoke screen made by the cigarette between his lips. "Mr. Woodson. You wouldn't be interested in becoming a motel owner"? He gave the young man a sly grin.

"No, no. Grew up in a place similar to the smaller towns around here. Just thought I'd check out the market." Know one thing, some pretty sassy babes selling Real Estate around here." He gave the manager a wink, turned and butting his suitcase against the screen edged outside.

Walking toward his car, he spoke to himself. "Sassy and sweet tasting too"! He laughed aloud. Inside the car he removed the business card from the visor. He pressed it on his nostrils inhaling deeply. Then licked it with his tongue.

"Marie, honey, there nothing like the taste of perfume in the morning. 'Midnight Passion,' I believe she called it."

# Introduction

Marie Pearson tied strings of four white and purple balloons together before attaching them to the arrow-shaped "HOUSE FOR SALE" sign nailed to the bark of the masterful oak standing at the corner of Plymouth and Short Street.

Assured they'd hold in the soft breeze she returned to her dark blue Lexus. After backing from the curb, she turned down Short Street for number sixty-nine, a beige with white trim colonial adorned with maroon shutters. This where she, the homeowner's chosen Realtor, would spend the afternoon hosting an open house.

The driver who was observing her from inside a shiny-clean deep grey Mercedes parked a hundred feet up on Plymouth Street slowly pulled away.

The sun reflecting off the Mercedes chrome flashed across Marie's rearview mirror causing her momentary glance. Smiling hopefully that perhaps this car carrying a prospective buyer en-route to the same house. Although it early, she thought.

Nothing worse, she pondered, than spending four hours on a Sunday afternoon alone, and if no shows, the desire to close it up early. That though would go against the seller agreement, and, as proven in the past, that one solid buyer could show in the final hour.

She was excited as always at the potential of a high commission which would help pay half of the first year tuition at Smith where her daughter was enrolled for next fall.

Little did she know then that her life insurance policy would provide far too soon. .

# Chapter One

Not too close now. Let her unlock the front door and slip inside to prepare for the opening.

Don't want to appear as an over-anxious buyer. After all, she could up the asking price, chuckling in appreciation at amusing himself.

For the past few months he had staked out similar open houses. The experience concluding, surprisingly, that rarely do buyers arrive during the first half hour. His reason for arriving forty-five minutes early. He parked along a wooded area just beyond the home.

Marie glanced nonchalantly in the direction of the slowing car, nodding a smile before key-coding the lock box. And, feeling optimistic at someone arriving early. Well, looks like just a ride-by. They may be turning around

His gloved hand gripped the steel blade easing it into the jacket inside pocket. His left hand lay resting in his lap touching the growing hardness inching along his thigh. Easing out of the car to kneel a few feet into the trees, he watched her skirt tighten as she bent to unlock the door. He whispered aloud. "Yeah, un-lock it beautiful. I'm right here waiting to place my best offer."

Not an hour later, Detective Jim Paulson and Mendelson Police Chief Joe Broderick stood inside the foyer exchanging observations of the crime scene, filling questionable event sequences with speculation while Plymouth County Medical Examiner, Dr. Tim Baker, completed his initial examination, jotting down notes on a legal-sized pad.

He replaced the plastic covering Marie's face and stood, a sigh of disgust exiting his mouth. "My wife works for her part time you know. Does clerical stuff in her office two days a week. Schedules appointments, type's closings, that type of thing. She likes her a lot. Going to take this hard, as will many."

Dr. Baker covers the Counties five towns, but lives in this small town of Mendelson.

His supplementary info describing Marie breaking a silence. "A widow you know. One child. A daughter, a high school Senior. Husband John passed two years ago, only forty-two. An aneurism I think it was. Started dating recently, but Amy is, or was, her life."

He took in a breath. Releasing it, head bent staring at the covered body. "She didn't suffer, but, poor soul, experienced terrible fright, as you both probably observed in her eyes. Wrought with terror. Facial expression frozen in the fearful realization of her last moment."

"Best guess scenario right now? She opened the house around noon, and not long thereafter, forced to have sex upstairs, or right here, while she lay passing out from blood loss. All within maybe twenty minutes."

Removing his gloves, turning to Detective Paulson. "I detect a slight odor likened to alcohol cleansing swabs. Our killer may have forgotten a condom requiring wiping her down leaving that light film you see dried to her hands, stomach, thighs and crotch areas. I'll better determine tomorrow in the lab."

Well, I'm out of here. I'll perform the autopsy tomorrow morning, results around eleven. But call first before just showing up. That'll save me listening to you moan and groan when it's not done," he said over his shoulder, black bag bouncing off his right thigh with each step.

Chief Broderick's "thank you Mark," trailed after the doctor. Those first words spoken by the Chief or Detective in ten minutes.

Twenty or so curious on-lookers gathered behind the yellow tape around the front lawn made a path for the doctor, some whispering their greeting. Others hoping for a reply to their whispered queries of what happened. He didn't respond.

Marie's body lay in its own pool of red, shiny by the overhanging candelabra.

There were three cut points. Throat, and each wrist. Her body remaining where killed, and visible to anyone about to enter the front, or peering through the small windows lining both sides of the door.

Detective Paulson reflected. Not only was this home on display today, . . . So too was Marie Pearson. He placed the printed business card he removed from between Marie's two fingers into an evidence bag. Holding it up to the light he studied the inked letters, ...NUMBER ONE.

The call had come in from a cellular phone used by a Michelle Locke and her husband Ben who took over the phone after his wife went to her knees on the lawn nearly passing out. She was first to witness the bloody scene after pushing in on the already ajar front door. According to her husband she walked into the foyer first voicing an echoed "hello" before reeling back screaming into her husband arms.

Chief Broderick motioned an instructional wave of his arm to two men from the county lab indicating they could secure and remove the body to the morgue.

Jim was in mid-sentence that he was going to contact the family when Joe held up a hand.

"While outside a moment ago I called Principal Anne Cushing notifying her of this tragedy and that I'd be at the school shortly. She'll have Marie's daughter's teacher bring her to the office where she would tell her this horrific news. She'll have the school department psychologist there as well.

She didn't think there were any relatives living in the area.

The Chief had been through this many times before. Although this being the first situation of this type in town since Chief. Most instances it was someone's Dad having suffered a heart attack. Or a Mom, a sister, a brother killed in an auto accident or on the job. At least then, one could count on a relative or close friends to be there as he broke the news.

He secured the crime tape across the front door leaving the two crime lab people inside to complete their work undisturbed. He walked toward his cruiser nervously lighting a cigar disregarding questions from the local newspaper and neighbors.

Just before reaching the car he stopped and turned. "You can see by the crime tape that this is an ongoing crime scene. It is early into the investigation and family members must be notified. When the time right, I will personally provide you with information."

Most there were familiar with Joe and respected his word. So aside from a few gasps, came whispers. "Thanks Joe," and silence, returning his courtesy.

The Mercedes pulled off rural Route 105 onto a narrow old farm road that dead-ended a hundred yards at the edge of a pond. An abandoned pump house formerly supplying water to the now weed infested cranberry bogs, stood slanted to one side and rotting.

The driver got out walking to the hidden side of the shed startling two Mallards resting at the nearby ponds' edge, sending them skipping atop their watery runway to flight, and several chipmunks to scurry from beneath a pile of old boards.

He carefully unzipped and removed the blue full body work suit laying it on the ground, followed by the ball cap, latex gloves, and saran wrap from his shoes. Kneeling he folded them in a neat roll before weighing them down with a large rock. He stood turning to walk to his car, head pivoting robot-like side to side studying the landscape. Reaching in the open driver window he pressed the trunk release there removing a small can. Returning to the shed spinning around slowly twice to give the field and surrounding brush and tree line a scan.

Pulling a leather glove onto his right hand and placing safety goggles over his eyes, he bent slightly cautiously pouring a clear liquid over the clothes. Immediately a small acid cloud rose above the pile causing him to step back escaping the fumes dissipating within seconds leaving only ash around the stone.

Re-tightening the container cap he placed it in the holder inside the trunk. Kneeling, he peeled three magnetic letters from the license plate before sliding behind the wheel and driving away.

Back home and feeling secure he lay on the sofa sipping from a cup of Honey Dew coffee turned cold. Feeling aroused his eyes closed. And as he does often, began talking with himself.

'Marie, always liked that name. Cute, pretty Marie Cummings in eighth grade, sparkling blue eyes, bright smile, breasts forming. And Marie White, living two houses away when in high school. Married, two kids, but oh so sexy in her tight jeans and low tops. I still see her purposely bending slowly and raising to arch her body in a stretch showing her bare waist line, and forming hard nipples against her see through top. This made me walk straight into a large shrub one day while mowing her lawn.

Marie Patterson continued to infiltrate his thoughts. That one Marie he so despised. That Marie possessing the ability to ignite his blood to the boiling point, and set his mind adrift in a whirlpool of frenzy.

Witnessing her final breath may not eliminate it, but it surely couldn't hurt. Why, oh why, did she not live in the goodness of other Marie's?

Not a fan of flight, two Dramamine tablets provided sleep through most of it. The touchdown in Atlanta was smooth. The train to Florida tedious. No I D's check though. And my flight to Atlanta could be for any reason?

A cheap motel by choice was found a block from the wharf area. Would do nicely? After all this was to be a short visit.

Checking the mirror, deciding I liked blonde highlights. And the large shades over my spray tan assuring I was no tourist.

Nathan spoke to his temporary companion. "That sure is a nice boat hey Poodle-girl.?"

Suddenly, there she was, standing tall and buxom, in her linen wrap-around covering a one piece yellow suit. "Tall bitch! Only one thing she's good for!" He looked down the dog. "Right, little girls?"

He stepped from the boardwalk onto the narrow dock. She stopped speaking to the young man and turned retrieving her cell phone. I drew closer turning sideways as if inspecting the other craft. My ears strained.

"No, I'm sorry, he's away until Wednesday. If it's a question about the boat, Carlo, the boat hand is here? Oh, okay, call back on Wednesday then."

She turned, " Carlo, remember to pick up extra ice at the store." She bent slightly, entering the cabin.

I continued past to the end of the dock. Carlos stepped off for the street. I turned landing my boat shoes softly on the wide planks arriving closer. I stood back listening. Can't assume she's alone? Might have another Papa inside riding her swindling ass, fucking him out of his insurance? His land? Whatever?

Aside from the sounds from two diving gulls squealing, soft waves splashing against the crafts, all was quiet. The moorings of other craft empty, but for one at the far end. The hair on my neck stood up. This is too perfect. After tying poodle-girl to the chain at the mooring two boat slips away, I walked as nonchalantly as I could gather up while counteracting the gnawing the pit of my stomach.

I stepped aboard, listening again. Stepping to the cabin door, gloves on, "Hello!" Anyone aboard?" Should another voice react, I could have my gloves off, and talk-up a story why I'm here.

I canvassed the dock and my exposure this side of the boat. All still. No one in sight.

In her shrill, uppity tone. "Who is it, might I ask?"

"A visitor to the boat down the end. Wondered if you know them? If when they might be back?"

A pair of flip-flops slapped the tile floor before clicking against her bare heels climbing the stairway. "So you're a friend of Mr. Goodman?"

As red toe nails of her right foot landed the top step, and forehead of bushy blonde hair appeared at the door frame, my hand grasped her throat slamming her just inside. "Hello, Ms. Patterson Almighty. Its pay-back time for conniving bitches like you! For Mom. For Dad. For . . . Our . . . My . . . Property?"

My hand released a bit. Didn't want finger indents or redness around her throat? Her face contorted in fear. Her lips moved to speak, "Is that . . . you Nath . . . ? Words cutting off, lost in gagging coughs as my arm went down hard, her head cracking against the brass.

On my knees, I ducked onto the cabin top stair, hugging it. I listened, hunched there for five full minutes. No voices, no screaming. Anyone coming to her aid. No Carlo.

My hand reached out over the waxed decking. The pulsating artery in her neck still. My head came up slightly, level with the deck, turning side to side scanning every direction. Set on both knees provided the leverage to push her limpness splashing for a final swim.

I stayed on my stomach, inching along the deck until reaching the two steps to the dock. I sat there just a second or two, just in case. No sounds, no questions. I untied Poodle-girl and walked slowly up the dock scanning windows, door ways, sidewalks.

The next morning, Carlo responded to a thumping sound against the boat. He looked down watching her head timely bumping the side with each wave.

I stood outside the coffee shop watching before stepping over to the policeman. "An accident, Officer?"

"Appears that way. You have a boat docked here? Acquainted the boat's owner?"

"Oh no Officer. I was walking past here yesterday though. Remember seeing a woman diving off for a swim. That's about it."

"You see anyone around this boat or on the dock here at the time you went by?"

"No, No one. Sorry. Just folks walking or milling around the street here."

"Well, at least I can throw a name down, as you said, seeing her diving. That following she either slipped, tripped, or whatever, while doing so." He jotted down on his pad.

"Anything else I'll get you at the Motel. By the way you couldn't find a better place than that flea-hole?"

"It suits my short visit. Didn't want to impose on my Uncle? Nights alone." A sly wink. "You know?"

The cop grinned. "Just in case you meet that friendly-someone, huh?"

"Plus they allowed the dog. I'll be leaving in a few days. Take care officer."

I strolled away. Anyone saw me yesterday hanging around, hopefully seeing me with Mr. Policeman today. No questions! And she had been diving!

It was back on Amtrak within the hour. "Coming home my sweet darling Maries', I've missed you!"

Marie, the realtor from the Short Street home flashed. So attractive. Although petite, sensually shapely especially when slowly ascending the stairway half-turning every other stair facing me to describe another trait of the home's character.

He rested his head back reliving his escapade . . . . . .

They entered the master bedroom as she continued spouting riddles of ceiling, wall, tapestry, and architect details. Spotting the master bath, I asked to wash my hands.

Inside I removed the thin body suit, gloves and shoe covers from inside my jacket. Stepping back into the bedroom she sat legs crossed on the edge of the bed. My hardness increased at her pose.

Suddenly her eyes grew wide. Smooth fore-head instantly frown-lined, awed at the site of my transformation.

Her mouth opened to question, but no words formed as she gasped a breath. Her breasts rose, my hardness swelling, a bulge visible to her beautiful blue eyes glancing down, bugging out in fright. Veins swelled at her temples, her mind grasping the reality that this house not what brought me here.

Marie felt her heart pounding within, his eyes intense, his mouth hanging open like an animal attacking prey. My god, my god, what is happening ! This isn't real! I just can't let,

. . . Legs came up clenched together as she rolled across to the other side of the bed. Her mouth opened wide to shout, words catching in her throat allowing only a hoarse, frightful cry. Thoughts ran frantically across her mind . . . why can't someone come in? . . . Where are they?

He was on her in an instant, muffled attempts to scream lost and silent in the heated air of her lungs. Kicking legs and wailing arms beat on the sides of his neck. His face became beet red, his face runny with sweat, salty droplets dripping onto her face, her lips. She tried to spit.

She shut her eyes hoping by eliminating his ghastly gaze she gains strength. He pinned her legs with his knees, his powerful arm coming hard and heavy against her chest. She winced in pain gasping for air, her body weakening.

She closed her eyes hearing his raspy growl, feeling the spray of spit, feeling cool steel pressed against her neck. remaining energy and fight draining, she imaged her own sweet daughter Amy within the frame . . . I love you my darling girl. Bewildered suddenly! She felt herself being pulled to the edge of the bed .

"Come," he growled pulling her to a standing position. Her legs limp from fatigue and fright bumped against each stair tread, pain stabbing her shoulder joint being pulled.

He dropped her to the hard marble tile in the foyer. Something in her body cracked. He leaped to the front door securing the lock. On her again, his large hand groped ripping away her blouse and bra in one swift motion. His hand reached down, panties tearing apart at the crotch.

Semi-conscious she heard his zipper and felt his hand hard against her, an odor of moist penis filling her nostrils. Vomit formed stinging her throat.

Eyes closed tightly she felt air from his arm motion sweep across her face . . . a warm ooze spewing from her throat. Her eyes flashed open but for an instant and for their last time.

His throaty gasps of sexual satisfaction timing perfectly with the feel of warm blood splatter, like wet beach sand hitting his plastic coat. "Yes Marie, yes," reverberating off the walls of the foyer.

Re-enactment complete, he rolled onto his side, eyes closing, lips moving. "Oh my Marie, can't wait till next time."

# Chapter Two

Chief Broderick stood in Principal Anne Cushing's office where she held Amy. One arm around her, the other hand brushing her hair as she sobbed uncontrollably.

The Chief stepped away to the window attempting to control the rage within that such people exist to cause such heartbreak. He caught sight of Mrs. Baker, Dr. Baker's wife, coming up the walk.

Excusing himself, he went to greet her in the hallway to spend a few moments. She told him that she would sit with Amy awaiting for her Aunt Ruth McCall, Marie's sister, arrived from out of town.

The Sunday evening news broadcasts carried the story of her brutal murder and a brief outline describing her family and background. According to local police the investigation is ongoing with no known suspects, asking that anyone in that area on Sunday who may have observed anything unusual to contact the Mendelson police.

He laughed aloud before changing channels. "Mendelson P.D., that's a joke hey Lady." He got up from the recliner patting Lady's head. "A good girl. Want a biscuit?"

He talked to her endlessly, hesitating for a response before responding himself. He found her nearly ten years ago when walking through rows of shoulder high corn stalks. She whimpered hearing his approach. There she was, a yellow Lab sprawled on her side, dried blood caking her under-belly. He removed his hunting coat laying it on the ground, rolling her in it, tying the sleeves together around her. His truck parked too far to carry her. He secured his belt through the top button hole dragging her, stopping every now and again to rest. And giving her body a break from some bumpy terrain.

The local Vet operated removing several buck shot, two in her intestine. After only three days she was standing, and eating. Another two days and he brought her home.

Reading the lost dog ad in the paper, he ignored it, his mind holding the owner negligent and undeserving of her. Like a parent allowing a child to roam unattended.

"He's mine now. Automatic adoption," he reasoned. Mumbling. "How's this Pa, huh? My dog, like I always wished. No excuses of yours to listen to."

His Father and he went back and forth over differences from when he reached twelve. Especially after Mother died. He adored her.

Wishing to escape those times, he returned to focus on today. "No time for that nonsense girl."

He and Lady were nearly inseparable. That is around the house and property. The car and truck were off limits. Except on rare occasions. Dog hair didn't belong on leather seats, wiped weekly with Amoral.

His eyes focused following down the columns of the Gazette real estate page. He concentrated the black marker, circling three open house ads upcoming this weekend. The back of his head fell against the leather, a smile forming on his face, fingers slowly massaging Lady's coat.

Awake suddenly! His mind's alarm clock clanging. The antique New Haven wall clock chimed. He counted. "Shit!" He jumped up racing to the shower. Forty-five minutes to get to work. Quickly drying and dressing he threw on his uniform greens, as he called them.

He would arrive at Monument Hospital just in time for his shift. He normally arrived a good half an hour early. He had made a good impression since starting there, and didn't want tardiness, or anything to mess it up.

He applied there after his return to Mendelson. The fine recommendation from Liberty Hospital in Virginia helpful. He enjoyed being a male nurse assistant. He often cursed himself, envious of his male R.N. counterparts. He regretting having given up continuing to study for his certification.

Though he still thoroughly enjoying his work. The hospital atmosphere. Caring for the ill.

His father seemed disappointed at his choice of work. Too damn bad. Mother more supportive.

That was long ago. Before his sexual appetite heightened. The Playboy magazines hidden in the barn. Dances at the Junior High forbidden in his mind since that first experience. Sally and Mary making up excuses for not dancing with him, haunting him to this day. He sat at home while classmates had their good times.

The same rejection followed him through Mendelson High. All that talk of the Junior and Senior proms. The expectations, the planning of parties. He watched T V, or played C D's through them all. He replied to Mother's comments of prom plans with excuses of his own.

Now he would have only beautiful women. They would appreciate him at last. They're last.

Sex bonding now, tied with vengeance. What a thrill beyond thrill. He would hurt no more!

No more rejection! No more stealing the land that should have been his!

Joe Broderick and Jim Paulson huddled side by side, heads bent, re-examining the crime scene photos spread out on the table inside the Chief's office. Both intensely focused. Waiting to see. To have some visual they had missed jump-out at them.

Thus far no witness had come forward and nothing of physical findings from any source at the crime scene, or during the finite examination by Mark Baker of Marie's body.

Heads unmoving, each muttered to the other every now and again, holding focus to every detail of each picture, the small magnifying glass held by Jim moving meticulously back and forth.

Joe finally stood arching his back in a stretch "Either our killer has done this before, or is a meticulous planner. Certainly fortunate in having no other buyers happening by. Or is that part of this psycho's game? ...The thrill of nearly being exposed."

Jim straightened rubbing his eyes and walking to the coffee urn. "During the weekend I went over the scene in my head again and again. I returned to the house and walked through a couple scenarios.

I believe this killer entered with her welcome, as a prospective buyer. She was showing him, . . . or her, around. They went upstairs and there in the master bedroom is where this maniac initially confronted

Marie as a threat. The rumpled bed linens, the broken lamp and all confirming this."

His hand scratched his forehead. "What really bothers me is why he didn't finish his attack upstairs. Maybe you're right Joe, part of the game. Psycho? No question there. Along with her body being left for anyone to observe in that foyer. And the business-card in her hand. We're dealing here with a real sick-o."

Joe's tone echoed impatience. "It's frustrating, not a single lead nor clue. And not one witness or neighbor with anything. Well, all in good time hopefully," as he went out front to answer his cell.

He hollered back at Jim. "Got to go, an SUV just rolled-over on 44."

Four days after she was maliciously attacked and killed, Marie was laid to rest after a funeral Mass at Saint Michaels. I sat near the back watching for the possibility that this looney should attend. I was introduced at the wake to her brother and two sisters. Her younger sister inconsolable then and at Mass sobbing loudly as Amy Armstrong's soprano voice beautifully sang the Ave Maria. Marie's daughter leaned on her Uncle, his arm around her shoulders the entire ritual.

Well maybe there is some comfort knowing she will be well cared for.

It was Sunday morning, the heavy rain had turned to drizzle, watching Lady bounding for the street to retrieve the Gazette. The sound of brewing coffee welcomed them back to the kitchen. Taking a cup from the strainer he shook it dry over the sink.

He spread the paper on the table open to the realty section to confirm the open houses as advertised in the Saturday edition were the same as today.

Seeing no changes, he picked up the folded Saturday edition with destinations already circled and headed to the car.

First stop, Evergreen Drive in Carver to observe. The Realtor contact person in the ad is Darlene Cassidy. Darlene, um, he thought, has a sweet sound. But you never know. Not Marie though. Well anyhow. Marie to me.

Three hours later he returned, pulling onto the long gravel driveway slowing before pressing the unique barn door opener he had installed, timing the glide-inside, touching the brake.

Another of his little games. He remained inside the idling truck until the door swung closed before silencing the engine. He stared at the real estate page folded on the seat. Two of the seven open houses in Carver and Mendelson hi-lighted in a yellow- marker.

He had been right about Darlene. But even better, he had under-rated his mind-set about Estelle Richards at the colonial on Miller Street in Mendelson.

Wow! His eyes closed, automatically starting the reel turning, flashing her on his imaginary screen. Lovely glossy blonde hair pulled back in a pony tail, dark colored leather skirt hugging firm hips releasing long legs, taut muscles eager to be bitten.

Her name should be Marie he thought getting out of the car and removing the blue coveralls from the shelf above the work bench. Tossing them in the trunk next to the real estate magazine open to her photo. He winked at her image feeling her presence there. "See you next Saturday."

She suggested to him that he call the number her business card she handed him. Her fragrance captured there, holding it to his nose, breathing her in.

Nearly two months had passed since Marie Pearson's murder. Local and county authorities were stymied. A the State police lab discovering nothing of advantage. One authority tried appeasing Chief Broderick that in most cases murders are solved with evidence or witnesses help. When there is none, you wait. You hope. You re-hash and, often discover.

The pacifying didn't help him feel any better. The town had for the most part resumed to near normalcy. Larger newspapers from surrounding cities stopped calling for updates. T.V. news only the occasional request for info. And the owner of the local Gazette told the Chief to call him should something develop. He wanted this solved, not just for his personal satisfaction, but for the family and the town.

Two local perverts listed on the sex-offender registry were questioned even though not regarded as, "The Type," preferring young boys in the past. But one never knows. They to could turn a different leaf, enhance their options.

Carver and Plymouth police had their suspicions of a Mark Tollman who had been jailed several years back for holding a female within his apartment for two days after picking her up at a bar. The rape charge didn't hold up for the numerous times they had sex, including in the men's room stall before they left the bar. The jury contending all consensual. Holding her captive with assault sent him away. He had a solid alibi that Sunday. And had been no problem, at least locally, during his five -year parole, or since. Of two others sought, one had died in a motorcycle crash, the second back in jail.

He poured his second cup from Mister Coffee into a travel mug, grabbed his duffle containing shoe bags, rubber gloves and tape, the tools of his new trade. Lady sensing his leaving  whimpered at being left behind. "There's food in the dish girl," patting her rump before closing the door behind him.

Estelle finished applying make-up talking to the mirror. "Shouldn't have had that third Cosmo dammit. But Frank had insisted. Of course he went off to play golf with Ted and Jack. He didn't have to look presentable to the public today. Not for them.

Looking pretty good she considered, reinforcing her ego at her full profile in the mirror.

She kept herself in good shape. Some credit going to Frank, insisting she go with him jogging and playing golf occasionally. A ten-minute stretching routine though, was her independent daily work-out.

"This will have to do," after a final glance of scrutiny. And she was out the door. First checking the trunk making sure it held the open house signs, and heading for 129 Miller Street.

# Chapter Three

He enjoyed driving the Mercedes for pleasure and speed. Mostly while driving on occasional longer jaunts. Otherwise, it sat idle in the barn. After humming and hawing to himself about it, he started the ignition. After all, he had read nothing in local or area papers any observations of vehicles around the Short street scene.

Turning left out of the driveway he felt a pang of paranoia momentarily. Whether they did know something, and their ploy to hide it. He glanced in the mirror confronting himself. Come-on, don't start with that. He shifted, pressing the pedal, accelerating to fifty in four seconds, engine purring like a kitten in this thirty mph zone. He quickly slowed eyeing Mr. Wiksten stepping to his mail box at the edge of the road.

Estelle lifted the sign from the trunk and leaned it against the bumper. Gripping the hammer, she pounded the sign post into the front lawn near the mail box.

Going inside she laid out copies of the house description and a log-in register on the kitchen table. The register information not only provided the owner she represented with the number of visitors, but herself with contact information, should she consider them of other properties.

That done, she carefully checked each room for appearance before lighting fragrance candles mixing the kitchen and dining room air with baking apples and cinnamon. A cozy ambience for visitors to inhale upon entering.

She inserted the CD she brought from home into the Bose introducing calming sounds of piano and violin. Leaving the slider open six inches, allowed fresh air in. She mentally took note that all was set before sitting at the table studying the brochure in readiness for questions.

Squatting down, he inched the slider delicately before peering inside. She sat at the breakfast nook now. Eyeing her perfectly toned calf exposed fed his eagerness. Her fragrance teasing his mind, toying with his concentration. He breathed her in nearly moaning aloud before catching himself.

Feeling the slider's guide-slot rubbing he stopped, choosing now to squeeze through the opening. Sliding one knee, then the other, crouching close to the nook and under the counter's overhang.

Quietly sucking in he held a breath momentarily releasing very slowly through the tiny oval of his lips. Patience, patience. She'll spot that leaf on the floor any moment bringing her to the patio to toss it.

She rose up questioning aloud as if the leaf to answer. "And how did you blow through such a small opening?" She bent squeezing the dried leaf in her fingers. "Dammit, in disgust as it broke into pieces on the floor, having to drop on her knees to get it all.

He surmised instantly her not going to come to him for his rise and grab. She in fact was making this too easy, hesitating as the tight short skirt inched up, baring nearly all of her smooth thighs. He couldn't contain himself another moment.

His boot baggy squeaked against the tile floor. Her head didn't respond a quarter turn before being in the grasp of his left arm, right elbow digging in her ribs, hand positioning the blade tight just under her chin, his rigid tone demanding silence.

The veins in her temples swelled, eyes bugging, heart instantly pounding in fright, thighs becoming wet. She had meant to go earlier.

His instructions were deliberate moving them to the first floor bedroom. Her legs turned to rubber. Forcibly shoved from behind, she landed face down, the bed-spread fabric burning her face. His knee stabbed into the small of her back forcing her to pee again.

She heard him sniff the air followed with a sigh of disgust before his knuckle whacked the side of her head, his throaty tone calling her a putrid bitch for wetting herself. His pudding treat won't taste the same. What was he to do now?

Groping hands ripped away her skirt, latex fingers probing. Suddenly her head snapped back his hand wound about her up-do, a stinging in her throat, a warm stickiness gagging her. She could neither cough nor swallow. Gargling blood, welcoming the shadows of darkness.

He pulled out of her, quick action snapping the condom. He scrubbed and probed in and around the area of penetration with high strength antiseptic and wipes with one hand, the other swabbing lips and tongue. Antiseptic replaced a pussy taste, muttering how sweet her juices were. So soft and hard she is in all the right places. He wanted her alive again, wiggly and warm.

Feeling secure with the scene, he paused, eyes of an MRI scanning every pore of skin.   Not wanting to leave this beauty just yet, but hearing the sound of heels on the walk, he bent over her corpse slipping the card between thumb and forefinger. He had reopened the front door just in time.  The sounds of the front door bell chime sending chills up his spine as he slipped out the patio door.

Chief  Broderick pulled to the side of Route 28 stomping on the brake, tires spitting stones into the air.

Dispatcher McCabe was continuing the broadcast requesting response to 129 Miller Street to investigate a call-in describing a body found inside the foyer. A Mike Carter called it in on a cell phone.

The chief  keyed his mike and advised he was responding. His heart quickened nearing 129 Miller observing the sign. He tapped his radio, "Hey McCabe! Tell Paulson it's an "open house."

Jim Paulson, eyes moving between plays of the N E Pat's game, and page ten of a new mystery novel balanced on his left thigh. Inches away salsa and chips balanced just above the knee, a bottle of Bud Light between his thighs. A clicker on his right thigh for channel surfing during the commercials.

His pretty wife, Audrey, sat legs curled a few feet away within reach of the chips while reading Nora Roberts. Naturally the telephone was positioned near her. Heaven forbid Jim be disrupted from his balancing act.

Despite his sigh she handed over the phone. "It's dispatch for goodness sake, she bantered back.

Careful not to disturb his lap collection he straightened just enough. Something's up, he now pondered. It's Sunday.  Sunday in Mendelson.

"What do you have Beth? You do know it is Sunday afternoon right. Just messing with you!" He added quickly before she gave him her good-natured sass.

"Chief just called in from Miller St, number 129. Said to tell you it's an "open house."

"Is that right?! Victim?"

"Female. Realtor, according to the caller. Chief sounds very excited. You better get a move!"

"On my way Beth, on my way."

"Sorry Hon, another murder looks like, right here in our small town. Probably be a few hours, depending," bending to kiss her cheek on his way to change clothes.

Jim parked two wheels on the lawn just as the Chief exited the front door. Eyeing Jim, he walked over bringing him up to speed with the scene. Jim shook his head now and again, clearing his throat, as was his habit before removing the cigar butt to spit. The Chief eyed the ground shaking his head at Jim. "We'll at least you've learned to turn your head away first."

Jill Anderson, a local reporter for the Gazette, leaned against her car watching them, eyes squinting in focused gaze attempting to transform lip movement to word. Knowing them both pretty well and when approachable and when not to, she'd let them alone until parting. Then the time to hit the Chief up first. Matter of courtesy really, being Chief, and the more approachable.

Whether it a suicide scene, motor vehicle or hunting accident, Jim be the go-to guy for the "gutsy" stuff. Descriptions of half naked and bloodied corpses, type info.

She knew it was his job, but he really liked rehashing those details. The Chief on the other hand observed and noted facts in his mind before separating and dismissing those gorier images.

Naturally murder scenes are a rarity for these men. Not the blood part, as observed by most officers over time Mangled body parts at accident scenes, the occasional suicide, or industrial accident.

Jill approached the Chief as he turned from Jim. "Jill, my sweet, thought you may have gathered enough reading our lips."

"Not all, Chief. From you maybe, but with Jim's cigar between his teeth, it's tough."

Not to be irreverent, the Chief swallowed an urge to chuckle.

"Well Jill, the realtor is Estelle Richards with Hallmark Realty in Bridgewater, where she and husband Frank call home. I imagine husband Frank, that is, immediately abandoned his foursome at Manomet Golf Club, and at this very moment is tearing across fairways and greens to reach his car in the parking lot.

Hands trembling, eyes bugging, mind spinning in disbelief at hearing my words over his cell phone after finding the number in her bag, along with a note he must have left her this morning before a heading for an early tee time. His words, 'meet me in the clubhouse lounge around 1:00 for a romantic lunch.' And, she thought enough of it to save in her purse. All indicative of a loving relationship .This is going to be rough."

Hearing this Jill's mind hesitated, recalling the heated argument earlier today with live-in Roger. Would she find what this couple obviously have?  Or at least had. And in the long run, would this husband find consolation in their special times?

She came back. "So Chief, is what you've seen or found so far similar?  You know, possibly related to the Short Street killing several weeks ago?  I mean two females, both Realtors, and hosting open houses?"

"Now Jill, don't jump ahead of yourself with assumptions. There should not be assumptions or presumptions in either police work or news reporting. You know that. So have patience.  I'll give you what I can when I can. You know that from our experiences."

He purposely hadn't mentioned the business card matching the first.

Jill finished penciling notes in her pad while walking to get her camera from the car, a sample front page photo and headline printing in her head to include, 'The Welcome Open-House' sign in the foreground of the house. How is it that tragedy and grotesqueness can at the same time, oddly enough, create that strange sense of excitement to a reporter? Sick, she thought, repositioning the camera on the seat.

A Lexus swerved partially onto the lawn tires pushing up the sod before stopping. The driver door remained open as the sound of cleated golf shoes clicked against the driveway identifying to the Chief and

Detective Paulson that this slim figured man is the victim's husband Frank.

Paulson moved to block the doorway raising his arms. These movements meant for brief consolation were lost as the husband conveniently sidestepped Jim sprinting through and into the foyer.

Jim glanced my way shrugging his shoulders in desperation before turning to follow knowing he would find him kneeling over his beloved wife gasping for breath, horrified and disbelieving.

And that is exactly how he found him. Jim's hand fell upon this despondent husband's shoulder signaling silent consolation before stepping back a few paces.

After five minutes or so Frank released his embrace gently laying his wife down, running his hand softly along her cheek before rising. It was another moment before he turned, a trembling hand extended to Jim.

Their exchange went from introduction to the person she was, the gruesomeness of the day. They parted when Frank left to follow the coroner people downtown. Jim told him to lock his car. He would have a cruiser drive him downtown and bring him back later.

The Chief joined Jim to re-walk the inside. They did so methodically while comparing notes.   Though both cognizant of the fact this the same killer, both hesitant to yet admit openly a serial killer in their community.  Joe closed the front door behind them and they pulled on their latex gloves tossing them into the brown bag against the bench on the lawn. They separated part way across the lawn, both heads moving back and forth, the Chief remarking, "clean, so damn clean."

He stood staring out beyond the bogs while the sound of burning short pine branches popped now and again devouring remnants of his killer apparel.

He loved it here in the quiet. This would have been gone too, sold off to fast talking Realtors representing greedy developers.

His father's arthritis crippling him more each year and mother's cancer, though slowed with radiation, weakened her physically. Her daily routine, a ritual.

Seeking answers, hoping for a miracle, the Father would roam the fields and woods he loved and had known for most of his seventy-one years. Mother and he would be better off living in a warmer climate. But he lamented leaving this place.

His mind became less and less aware and slowly dementia set in. Papers were signed, his signature barely legible. Why hadn't he called? Why.

Yes, I had left and visited in-frequently. But they to blame. Not me. Not Father. They will pay.

He sat on a log pile back rested against the peeling paint of the barn. He thought about painting it several months ago. Thinking on it later, deciding to let it peel awhile. This damn town will just appraise it higher increasing the taxes. The hell with them.

It was around three, the sun lowering now on this spot warming him. The contents from three empty Heineken bottles having relaxed him. Lifting up on the opener he snapped the cap off a fourth , staring at the small grove of apple trees, eyes closing on happier times . . . . . .

I heard the back screen door close. Looking up from my finger painting, a gift from Santa. "Coming love, coming. He sat next to me at the table. Painting looks about finished Nathan. And looks good too. Neat too, cause you stayed in the lines. Good work."

I smiled, happy at his words. Mother poured lemonade and sat admiring my work too. "You should try painting something without numbers." She turned to Papa. "We should pick up a canvas or two for him to try on."

"Good thought," he agreed, taking a long drink and smiling at me. "What do you think on that my boy?"

"I could try, I guess Pappa." He patted my back, "sure you could. Something else too. Time you started helping a bit round here. You know, a little hoeing in the garden, planting seed, that type of thing. You're nearly six you know."

Gee "Papa you think I could?"

"Sure enough. I started when I was five feeding chicks and so on. Pappa winked, "could be a little allowance in it too." He hesitated then, explaining what an allowance is.

"You mean my own money saved in a piggy bank? I could buy candy or a toy?" Looking at Mamma. "Or something for Mamma. And you, Papa."

The revving engine from the four-wheeler zig-zagging the trail the other side of the pond jolted him. His brief respite bringing a smile. How he missed, . . . cherished those good times. His dreams held more of the same recently. Happiness and bitterness creating an angry mix.

Oh Mamma why did you get sick? Papa, how could you get weak to be hog-tied and swindled by that woman? Fuck them! Feeling anger, he tossed an empty against the barn. "Fuck them. All of them." He thought of his Marie now. Smiling, feeling arousal. "You're all I have to look forward to, sweet Marie." When did this pain, anguish, intensify? He didn't care. The rush fed his appetite.

Word out of a second murder had media coverage increase reaching outlying areas, and a bleep on two national broadcasts. Boston and Providence stations broadcasting live from the scene or using the police station as backdrop. After four days it died down to just the local and area town newspapers following it until it went from front page to third and last.

After all, the victim not a celebrity. Just wonderful hard working fellow beings brutally killed, leaving bereaved loved ones heartbroken and destroyed. Some starlet or celebrity, even celebrating a sordid background, would hold media attention for weeks.

Totally disgruntled in the absence of witnesses and no conclusive physical findings, Joe swore at the wall while Frisbee-tossing the Gazette across the room.

# Chapter Four

Lost in thought, his forefinger played over a couple chin whiskers missed by the razor earlier.

It left his chin for the Rolodex, his other dialing in a number. "Could I speak with Dan Hudson please? This is Chief Joe Broderick, Mendelson, Mass. P D."

"Dan Hudson speaking, who's this again?"

"Joe Broderick, Dan. I'm glad you're in. And how've you been?"

"Hey Joe, great to hear your voice. Thought about you a few weeks back. Caught the news on Fox about a killing in your town. Was going to call, but, well you know? So what's happening with you, and with that?"

"Well everything is good with me, the family and all. These killings though. Well, that's just it. Not anything, a damn thing, in the way of evidence or witnesses. And that one you caught on Fox was number two.

First was nearly four months ago now. Was hoping we could meet, or for now I could send some file for you to look over? I've been mulling it over. Could use some help? I realize you don't have authority, but as a favor old friend."

They discussed both cases for half an hour during which Joe faxed Dan information and photos. Locking his office, he headed out feeling better. His mood on an upswing.

Dan was good, real good. Some locally, especially State wouldn't like his contacting Dan. From past experience requesting, or even suggesting outside help, bent their egotistical noses a bit. More importantly, to him anyway, he contended when a case gets cold, reach out.

He dialed home. "Hey Sweetie, what do you think about dinner out tonight? I'll call Pennes' for a six-thirty reservation." Anne, his wife of twenty years questioned, " What's the occasion? The Selectmen give you that raise promised you two years ago."

"Just want to take my girl out to dinner. Fix me a vodka martini. See you in fifteen."

Joe would talk with her at dinner about Open Houses, which she occasionally hosted.

Anne stirred Joe's Martini before sitting back down at her desk to reschedule her appointments. She sold real estate part-time for a broker in Plymouth. She could work in Mendelson, but somehow felt more comfortable dealing with attorneys, bankers and others in Plymouth who didn't have to deal a police chief's wife, and asking her police related issues.

Hearing familiar footsteps on the porch, Lady's head appeared in the window. "Good, Lady.

Sit now, I've had a busy day." He opened the frig grabbing a beer with one hand and a plate of scrambled hamburger mixed with corned beef hash with the other. Lady sniffed, immediately sitting.

Nathan placed the full bowl down before settling into his favorite leather. Popping the bottle cap and taking a long steady swallow, his head fell back, eyes closing recapturing each moment with her.

She was lovely. Skin soft white and smooth, smelling of a sensuous fragrance, even around her sweet little pie. She must have been planning something special with someone later. Beat him to it he thought now, smiling.

His hand slid to his crotch, pressing hardness. He had long wondered how the mix of perfume, and blood could arouse? Is he sick? . . .How? Lady-girl stirred, lifting her head at her masters snoring.

Dan Hudson studied the crime scene photos again, rereading scrawled notes of what the Chief told him on the phone. His mind clicked like a computer program in profiler mode.

He penned the word. . . strength. Beneath, . . . male. Then, planning...then,. . . scheduled. It was a start. He dialed Joe to set up a date to visit Mendelson.

Four days later the Chief was treating Dan to breakfast at Dave's Diner on Route 28. Afterward they would visit the Short street scene and move onto the Miller Street scene. Though both addresses no longer reflective of anything near a murder scene, Dan wanted to visualize.

The sellers still living there since the murders were not too pleased. Realizing that the word out about the murders wasn't helping. And the reason, PRICE REDUCED letters appeared on for sale signs.

Chief Broderick watched Dan walk the house interior slowly, methodically stopping now and again, studying photos of that day. He exited the house pacing the yard, then both sides of the street. It was like following a ghost walking in a killer's footsteps.

He stood across the street squatting momentarily sifting the fallen leaves with his hand.

"I can feel him here," he said aloud. "Watching. Waiting for the right moment, anticipation growing within, beads of sweat popping out on his forehead, sexually aroused perhaps."

Dan paused, looking at Marie's real estate ad photo. "She certainly a beautiful woman. Could be motive of some kind, his selecting attractive victims? This could also attribute to time passing between episodes. Time for selection. Time needed to form his ideal victim. Her build, hair style,  or eye color? The name perhaps? Whatever his sick mind and motive makeup.

# Chapter Five

She hesitated momentarily before stepping from the curb. A breeze blowing in her direction lifted the knee length silk skirt, static cling holding it in place, revealing her thigh. With both hands holding bags, she turned her hips, raised her right leg wiggling a bit, and finally it fell into place.

She appeared more beautiful than the first time I spotted her leaving the realty office over on Pine. My eyes followed as she ran several steps, breasts heaving aside exposed cleavage flirting with oncoming cars. Bending slightly she placed two shopping bags temporarily on the trunk while searching for keys in her pocket book. She prematurely hit the auto trunk release. Her arms thrust forward one hand grasping a bag but not in time for the other spilling grocery items onto the sidewalk.

My chance, unexpected as it is. "Move, move you idiot" he urged himself.

"Can I help"? She looked up eyes studying suspiciously for a moment. "Well, um, maybe you could just pick up those cans in the gutter there," nodding in direction. "Thank you so much," as he returned them to the bag in the trunk.

Pearled teeth set in soft-pink gums, breathe hinting the piece of gum sitting on her tongue spearmint flavor. I bent picking up another can, eyes focused on the lean calf muscle tightening as she leaned into the trunk.

"You're a realtor, I suspect," nodding at her license plate, HSE-4-SALE

"Nearly ten years now", she advised.

Prolonging this opportunity. "Sellers or buyers market right now? See lots of signs around."

A vivacious smile edging on the provocative, "In my business it's always a buyer's market. Thinking this way keeps me positive. Well I must drop these at home before a noon appointment," her automatic smile flashing, eyes calling . . . "Thanks again."

Before able to conjure up a suitable response, her door closed and the engine started.

Tempted to follow, he held back, for it wasn't at her home that Ms Janine Shepard and he were to meet again.

Exhilarated, he sprinted to the car parked behind Staffer hardware, climbing in laying back against the head rest. Feeling arousal, he slid a hand under my belt and down. Eyes closed, her image lighting up before me, smiling, outstretched arms beckoning me closer, closer. He buried my face between her heaving breasts inhaling her fragrance splashed over freshly showered skin, turning me euphoric with each breathe. He arrived home, no memory of the road.

Inside he wanted it to last, laying on the couch unloosening his buckle. Done, he studied his Mother's photo, "Mamma, good mamma. He paid, now they'll pay. You were happy here, loved this place. So did I. Pappa was weak, blind to it all. He set her framed photo back in its special place.

Dan Hudson pulled his Bronco to the curb in front of the Mendelson police station. His watch told him he was forty-minutes early. He left the car there walking back around the block to where he passed Katie's Place. If he read the sign right you could get the Best Breakfast in Plymouth County, 5:30 am-10:p.m.

A bell rang overhead with a push on the door. Been awhile since stepping into a place with one of those he thought. Scanning five booths and a counter of ten stools, he opted for the one empty booth, sliding in and flipping the plastic menu open.

A voice bounced lightly off the tin ceiling. "Coffee"? Turning over his shoulder, eyes caught the smile of a shapely blonde stepping from the counter toward him. Her short black skirt hugged firm thighs, and unrestrained breasts jiggled behind a thin white blouse.

My inner voice complimenting, "did you pick the right breakfast spot or what?"

She stood but a second as her right knee found the bench cushion. Leaning forward she poured a  steaming brew, while introducing two pointy nipples.

Her hair was light brown with blonde highlights styled in a short butch-cut standing straight up. Not a style I find appealing, but on her looked good, provocative even. Her smile was friendly lined with slightly crooked, very white bottom teeth.

"Thank you, young lady," I said closing the menu.

"Wow, a gentleman, right here in Mendelson. Let me freshen up four or five cups and I'll be back to take your order."

Even a priest be tempted to glance at her perfect butt maneuvering between tables, tightening when she paused to pour. If her glance in the mirrored wall caught someone looking, a slight grin and momentary eye contact said thank you. And it's mine all mine.  Something, I surmised, she had encountered a thousand times before.

"So my gentleman friend, what can I get for you?" Before he could speak.  "Corned beef hash? Best anywhere. That is if you like hash." Her left knee found the cushion again, she arched her shoulders back as one might to stretch a tired muscle.

Open to this observation, "Tired this morning?"

"Why yes I am. But what else is new.  Seems I'm always tired. Think it's time for a new mattress, or something? . . .Maybe vitamins. What is it you want?"

"I'll have the number two. Eggs over medium, bacon, wheat toast. And you can top off the cup while you're here, thank you."

She finished writing, slid the pencil in her hair and sauntered behind the counter without a word. After my second observation, man that is one sweet . . . . .

"You're going to be blind doing that," a snickering Chief Broderick heckled, sliding onto the bench facing me.

My mouth opened, but he beat me. "Yes she is, and a single mother of a fifteen-year-old daughter.  And a real good gal. Doesn't fool around you should know,. . . well dates every so often? So don't let her sensuous exterior give you the wrong impression. Makes for good tips. Especially for those horny guys trucking on through. She's a hard worker, and a good mother.

Jimmy, her high school steady, and the dad, moved away after college. Visits now and again. His family moved on too. So she continues raising Angie pretty much on her own. Both her parents died in an accident ten years ago. I'll never forget knocking on her door that night.

So, I saw your car in front of the station and figured you might be here. What brings you back so soon?"

"Simply to visit a while. Look around, drive around. Get a bit familiar with each crime scene again, and the area. Sometimes spending time in a place puts the mind at ease. You don't feel like you're rushed. And, believe it or not, ideas and theories come forth to mind, almost like infusion. In some cases only one, maybe two decent ideas focus that way. Other times they just ravel out in front of you. The latter the nearer scenario, but you don't know until you experiment. Sounds goofy to you Chief?"

"A little, to be honest. But you're the guy with the in depth background, seen hundreds of cases in your time. I didn't call you in on this simply to get reacquainted

If this killer is from the area, I along with others could miss things that may register with a fresh mind, like yours."

Squinting at the name tag as she set the plate down. "Thank you Jen."

Chief will verify that I prefer being called Jennifer. Right, Chief", setting down his cup of tea. "He knows my name. I know he likes tea. Enjoy, gents."

I reached for the pepper shaker trying hard to keep eyes on my plate with the Chief here. He smiled, "go ahead, take another gander. I'm looking the other way."

After finishing breakfast we walked to the station where I gathered additional info and pictures before setting out for Pembroke, three towns away. Here I would store my car to lease another. One never sure who is who, and whether that who is watching. Or is it whom? This drove both me and my eighth grade English teacher, Mrs. Dwyer, crazy too.

Dan could feel himself settling in now, the return of that old familiar sensation, somewhere between a rush and anxiety. Come on! You a heinous bastard. Come on. Drop something. Any clue.

That guy sitting with the Chief likes her ass too. Wonder who he is? Yes, Jen Baby, you could be a Marie? A little too tough on the exterior, but could be well considered, sighing as her skirt lifted exposing more athletically-toned thighs. That part of you is all Marie. If she was only in real estate.

The sale complete with passing of papers, Janine left the Harbor Savings Bank for her office. First though she would stop at her bank, Citizens One, and cash the $11,000.00 commission check. Her savings would get $10,500.00, and then it was home to clean house in preparation for the cocktail party she was hosting tonight. She did this every six to seven weeks for close friends and working associates. Once or twice a year she would also invite a few local town officials, police and fire chief, and selectmen. This was one of those times.

An excellent cook, she normally prepared a dinner party of six or eight herself. These times though she called upon Simon Legrange, owner of Simon's Catering in Plymouth. He would prepare and lay out a nice combo buffet of seafood and beefy items, and supply a bartender and the right wines.

She hummed along to a CD, Jazz for a Quiet Afternoon, while dusting and vacuuming the foyer and living room before moving to the more spacious dining room lengthened from sixteen to twenty-four feet two years ago and adding French doors leading to the twenty by twenty outdoor two-tiered patio and over-hanging arbor sitting areas.

She loved entertaining, handsome commissions allowing this pleasure. She remained single through several enticing relationships, two of which included tempting proposals.

She opted for her remaining independence, "Mr. Right", as her mother would say, yet to show himself. Her belief mounting that would ever happen.

She had three real close friends, a sister living in New Mexico with husband and two daughters with whom she exchanged visits three times a year. A cousin and aunt or two with whom she shared Holiday cards and an occasional phone conversation.

She worked as an agent for five years before venturing into her own business maintaining her sole agent status and a secretary working from a small office on Main Street next to the Library. She had a growing business and loved every minute.

When overwhelmed she called upon Ursala Hendricks, a mother of three willing to accept a moderate per diem, and a three percent cut of a sale. If the Ursala option unavailable she didn't mind handing off a client to Maggie at Colonial Realty whom she considered a good friend and had worked with before.

Her head lifted from sweeping the tile observing a gray car parked across the street, more in front of the neighbor's property. A Mercedes, she thought, squinting through sun's rays. Couldn't tell if anyone seated inside? Turning, she heard the engine idling.

The homeowner had mentioned that the next neighbors, the Pattersons, were away for two weeks visiting their son in New Hampshire. Visitors to the open house could therefore park in front. Cautiously she stepped to the bottom of the patio scanning their back yard and porch through the arborvitae. She saw nothing and continued down the side of the property toward the street.

Running steps pounded the pavement suddenly. A door slammed. She ran now only to see through spaces in the high hedge-line flashes of the Mercedes racing away.

She felt a bit startled somehow, questioning whether to take the precaution and call the police. She thought of checking next door. Common sense convincing her against it, she ran back inside.

Within five minutes she heard a car door close, and recognized Patrolman Snyder in the driveway. After asking some preliminary info he proceeded to check all doors and windows from the outside and walked the perimeter of her property and two abutting.

He feeling satisfied all seemed intact and no evidence of intrusion observed, Janine started apologetically speaking of acting too hastily, to which Snyder made a point that it's always best to call. He was gone within twenty-five minutes.

Feeling more at ease, but not completely she poured a half glass of a Chardonnay before settling in the corner of a sofa turning the cover of a recently published Nora Roberts.

He threw Lady a dog biscuit before settling into his chair to watch the six-o'-clock news. The newscaster's lips were moving but it was as if the volume was muted.

It was not the reporter he saw but the image of Janine Shepard, her lips moving in unison with the reporter's.

His mind in a replay of the night he stalked her at home. She came in the side door scuffing her shoes on the entry carpet. I thought, what a nice little girl, well bred and taught to keeping the house clean. She moved gracefully into the kitchen tossing her keys onto the counter before climbing the stairs to her bedroom unbuttoning her blouse with each step letting it slide down her arms as she entered the bedroom flipping it onto the bed before going into the bathroom, and turning on the faucets to the tub.

I became hard instantly watching as she unbuttoned the black slacks which fell to her ankles followed by light purple panties wriggled off her hips slithering slowly down toned thighs and calves to the carpet where she toed and flipped them onto the bed.

My breathing was quickening. I began to throb. I had to focus, force myself into leaving before it overcame me. I had to keep to plans. It couldn't happen here.

I slipped out the narrow opening back onto the terrace. Tapping gently while pulling on the thin metal plate on the inside latch to lock back in place. A dog started barking beyond the hedge of the neighbor. A door opened and the owner called out to dog.

I ducked into the hedge watching and listening for five minutes before stepping quickly to the sidewalk, and then nonchalantly strolled around the block to the Mercedes.

I closed my eyes watching her again and again. She was consuming me. It had to be soon.


Dan drove Main Street parking out front of Alba's Convenience Mart. He wanted to pick up an area map having forgotten to ask the Chief for one. The lay of the land, rural roads, ponds, rivers, . . . all important. Locals, maybe like Alba here, going through her daily routine, noticing things, people, while not really thinking about it Full of subconscious information though when led correctly.

"So, are you Alba?" No I'm Michelle, her sister. You need her for something? We live next door. Or perhaps I could help you."

"No, no I was just putting a face with the name of the store."

"Just a curious sort, huh, she retorted. Can I help you find anything?"

"A map, local area map, if you have any."

"Down the end of this counter in that rack, just above the girlie mags, which would be more interesting perhaps," a statement offered along with a long hoarse laugh and a deep chested cough indicative of her smoking.

Dan chose a map after unfolding and folding. "Just the map, thanks. Had enough of those when I was fifteen?" Figuring that Michelle a sport, "the real thing is better."

This drew another hoarse chuckle from Michelle as she took his ten and fingered the register for his change.

He ignored the look in her eye ,and her remark," know what you mean." She then recanted almost apologetically, "I didn't mean anything. I'm so use to joking around with the regulars."

" Michelle, don't be. I started it. You seemed like a sport. Nothing intended."

Michelle's hand came across the counter, "One buck and three cents change."

"You need the map cause you just moved into town? I can direct you if you need? Tell you where to enjoy a decent meal, find a dentist, you know. I'm generally not this talkative, but you're my first customer and the store is empty. You are an early bird."

Dan waved his hand at the change, "Keep that, consider it a surcharge for the comedy. And yes, I might be. Nice to see you." And I was out the door heading down the street for coffee ,and with luck, having Jen serve it up.

With one foot in the door, "Well, starting your day early. Coffee regular?" Her voice a near echo of airiness.

"And a good morning to you Jen."

"Remembered my name. That's a plus," her sultry voice making one feel at home, green eyes piercing before leading me to a booth, standing close as I slid in .

" Busy day? Up and at ems, " speaking softly now.

" Nothing special. I'm an early riser."

"Early to bed? Isn't that part of it?"

" It is." And not desiring at least for now to take it further, I ordered just English toasted. After twenty minutes and scanning the local Gazette, I left money with the slip on the table and left.

Consciously I looked around to say a good-bye, but she was in the kitchen. She certainly one appealing lady. "Get a move on" the command to himself.

There he goes. Mmm, looks like sweet Jen has a follower. Wonder if he has a connection with the Chief? Maybe just an acquaintance. Can't be too well off, driving a '98 Camry.

Seeing Dan opening a map onto his steering wheel and dash, he pondered now, new in town, visiting? This might require some watching. Ah come on Nathan told himself, no time for paranoia.

Jen finished her shift at 1:00 tossing her apron in the laundry bin before heading for home , and the hot bath she visualized for the past hour, hoping relief from aching legs, and to ridding her skin the smell of kitchen grease.

She lay in the tub head back on a folded towel, Emmy Lou Harris' version of Crazy filtering in from the player in the bedroom.

She took in a long drag allowing the smoke to trail slowly. She only smoked one or two a day now, times like this her favorite.

Seems like a nice guy really, thinking of her earlier customer. Not bad looking either, handsome even. And distinguished, but only moderately so, with graying temples. Strong cheek bones and green eyes deeper set than most that sparkle from their little caves. Nose slightly flattened on one side, maybe he was a fighter, or a football player with those wide shoulders.

Wonder who he is? What he's doing in town? She remembered now, the other day, he was sitting with Chief Broderick. Mmm, sucking in the last drag and tossing a two pointer into the toilet. He shows again I may just make it a point to find out.

# Chapter Six

Dan drove the outskirts of town starting at the Carver line, maneuvering as best he could the Routes 44 and 106 areas, and rural roads off each. He stopped three or four times already, driving where passable and walking-in one time to an area of small ponds.

He'd worked many cases in the past within similar places as this. Funny, whether in Alabama, Connecticut, or right in Mendelson, or New Hampshire, in one way or another, just about the same. Thinking about what his Dad always said, " Most places are pretty much the same. It's not where you live but what you make of it." And he was right.

Dan had his routine. He would meet with local authorities for info on known locals who had records of sexual assault, and so on. He did his own thing. And yes had offended local authorities in the past without really being aware of it after being offered some field assistance. On several occasions in the past, when made aware of it, he'd apologize, explaining simply that he preferred to work certain areas of a case solo.

At other moments, Dan had blatantly told an over zealous "rush the case sheriff or chief " simply to let him be. Following with, "if I need you, I'll let you know" remark, conveyed in his "don't screw with me voice.

Joe Broderick wouldn't interfere. Like now, having seen me only twice. He knows that if there is the need, I'll see him. I also realize that if I don't check in once a week or so he'll get jumpy and call for an update. And that's fine.

Joe and he were in the Marines together, through boot, Da-Nang and back. He was wounded and got out before Dan. Kept in touch, being in enforcement and all.

I wanted the prestige and adventure, so to speak of the FBI, he his hometown girl and being a member of the local police force. I often thought his choice better than mine.

The travel and transfers from one office in one state to another sometimes occurring within five years of another took a toll. When single it was exciting and for me challenging, wanting new case experience and opportunity to move up in the ranks.

Jill and I were married in September of 1974. After two kids and four transfers it ended in 1981. We had slowly become strangers? I loved my work. The challenge, excitement. Most guys, and women, were single or had no kids. I should have made more of an effort in demanding less travel and in assignment selection. It was I, all me. I still love her to this day. Well, a caring love anyway."

"She remarried five years later. I met him a year or so after and have been in his company several times at family gatherings or a relative's wake or two. An auto mechanic of all things. Owns a very busy garage, has done well. A decent, hard-working guy. I learned this after checking him out when I learned she was seeing him.

My son and daughter and the grand kids visit more often now since I retired after twenty-five years.

Being in my private agency now four years with my partner Mike, also a former Fed and good friend.

Do a substantial business screening prospective employees for larger companies. Oil, financing, brokerage firms mostly. Don't want the loss or the embarrassment by an employee of an unscrupulous situation if they can prevent it. Also investigate suspected embezzlement situations, doing undercover for a couple Fed agencies, and occasionally what I'm doing in Mendelson.

We don't do a lot of it though. As a favor mostly, as in this case. Though certainly not pro bono, for sure.

We aid the locals with tracking and evidence gathering mostly, often so very discreetly. Once in awhile coming forward for court appearances.

A mistake I allowed was talking to Joe that day at the diner. It may have gone unnoticed, or hopefully observed as just another guy talking to the Chief.

But you never leave things to chance, so the story is, I'm contemplating a move to the area and simply checking out the local real estate.

Enough of this for today. Wonder what's on the supper menu at Dave's.

Damn! It slipped my mind all day. The Chief asked me to join his family for dinner tonight. I'll pick up a nice bottle of wine at the liquor store across from my motel.

Janine walked to the end of her driveway reaching into the box holding the Sunday Gazette. She sipped from her coffee cup pausing to look up the street, as was her habit, one way then the other before slowly retracing her steps, head down reading the headlines.

She set her cup on the bannister of the side porch. She breathed in the fresh morning air stretching her arms facing the sun feeling the warmth wash over. A robin splashed creating circles in the bird bath, a squirrel hopped the lawn, a nut hatch pecked the bark for tiny prey.

She shrugged at the thought of sitting through such a perfect day at the rambling colonial on Lady Slipper Lane. She smiled to herself considering now that it does have a nice deck and patio area. She just may take advantage in between welcoming interested prospects.

After refilling Lady's water dish, Nathan picked up the Real Estate section of the Gazette. Scanning the second page he saw the ad and photo of the house and in larger print OPEN HOUSE-   SUNDAY, noon to four. Printed beneath, Exclusive listing with Janine Shepard.

Simply seeing her name in print conjured up images. Anticipating his plan, seeing her up close, touching her hair and skin at last. His eyes shut, chest pounding with exhilaration. A few hours, just a few hours.

Joe Broderick returned home with his wife from the nine-thirty Mass at St. Michaels. He hoped sincerely that saying four Hail Mary's and four Lord's Prayer would help his case.

St. Michael's where he had been an altar boy from age eight to twelve, and where he and Anne married. Kids all Christened there.

He thought of Father Paul. Six foot three, carrying about two-twenty, with hands of a blacksmith. Yet a gentle soul and nicer, fairer man one ever the good fortune to meet . . . and confess to!. At the end of his battle with prostate cancer he was down to one fifty. Like myself, most parishioners knew him for the fifteen years stationed here. Twice the Bishop reassigning him held back after being deluged with letters and calls from the Faithful of St. Michaels.

Joe made coffee while Anne changed into hanging around jeans and top. As sometimes with a Sunday, without plans, they would sit on the porch exchanging sections of the Sunday Gazette.

As had become Joe's habit starting after the second killing, he would scan the real estate section jotting in his head addresses with an open house scheduled. He had spent Sunday's driving past or parking down the street from some in his personal car, and on his own time.

As with such times the precautionary aspects once heightened in priority become lesser along with other demands. And too the anticipation of "maybe we'll get lucky" aspect weakens in time. Time has a way of lessening memory, hurt, desire. Then too it had been some time. Maybe it's done. He's moved on.

Dan had no such misgivings while scanning the same listings. Luck he knew had nothing to do with it. Well, his thought reconsidering, sometimes. Luck, or coincidence, if such a thing?

"Well hi there. Dan, right?", Jen's raspiness tone echoed.

"Yes, that's the name. Jen, right, Dan jostled.

"Don't you take any days off, Jen? A work-a-holic, huh?"

" A favor for Millie, Millie Simpson. She works here on Sunday mornings for some extra cash. She works five days at the mill store where they sell curtains and fabrics. Takes Saturday off to spend with her hubby. He's a special cop, you know, part-timer. Works Sunday, early shift so some regulars can have the day. Plans to get on regular some day I guess. I'm sure you didn't need that much info did you."

"No problem. If I write a book someday on Middleton, I'll be prepared. And, I like hearing you talk."

"Never heard that one before. So what will it be, Danny Boy?"

"Well I meant it, and two over medium, side of hash and wheat toast dry. And, if it's not busy, maybe you could sit a minute."

"Harry might not mind. We'll see okay?" The thought of wanting to crossed her mine walking to the kitchen, browsing around, hoping no one else came in. Be nice to sit and talk.

He spotted her car in the driveway. Signs stood in place near the street with balloons being tossed at the option of the wind.

He drove past edging to the side of the road close to where a patch of woods abutted separating the property from the home next door. Perfect. Acting like an interested buyer, he walked   nonchalantly up the side yard looking about studying the roof and siding.  Cradling his small bag, he crouched now in a small space between two over-grown arborvitae shrubs.

Listening intently, eyes focused on two legs outstretched on the lower half of a lounge chair, the rest of her concealed around the corner.

The garage doors were closed he had noticed. Slowly and carefully he took a few more steps. He had to be sure it was she.  And that the owner wasn't there. The legs though looked like those pictured in his mind

Yes, Baby it's all you. She was outstretched on the lounge eyes closed, hands folded on her lap unmoving, and peaceful. Her head lay back, sunglasses shading her eyes.

Perfect facial bones, chin, small ears and sleek neck. Breasts heaved slightly with her breathing.

The breeze unraveled the tan wrap-around skirt revealing her right thigh.

His heart started pounding as he set to approach. He would act surprised at seeing her there, and she surprised in turn, at which point his one man show would open.

A car door slammed shut. The sound came from the front driveway he thought. He stood frozen as one petrified. He had to move. Taking each step deliberately backward now, eyes glued to her when she suddenly sat up erect.  She heard it too.

She instantly twirled her legs off the lounge standing and adjusting her skirt while shaking her head squinting at her image in the window, fluffing her hair a bit before rushing through the slider toward the front door.

Kneeling now in the temporary shelter provided by the overhang of shrubs he clenched both his fists pounding the sod several times in a rage of anger and disappointment, swiping his coverall sleeve against his forehead collecting sweat along his brow.

Damn, fucking damn. His hardness-turned inch-worm instantly. A face appeared in the side of the Bay windows, eyes peering out over the window box of red gardenias. He arched further into his space the shrub stems sticking his back side. She was blonde too, the bitch. Have good looks, you wide eyed painted lipped freak-bitch? Messing with my day. I could make you pay, do you instead. Come on outside for a look.

He heard the slider screen slide open. He spoke softly at himself, his habit. "Wow, look at you. Platinum blonde up-do, sleek legs covered by white stockings. Red shoes, matching bag, big gold earrings and the sparkler on that finger. Whoa baby, turn, turn. Yes Mama, look at that v-cut blouse, a hint of cleavage creamy white."

A big guy, maybe six feet, handsome, nice hair, Italian shoes, followed her. His spotless and creased linen slacks hung perfectly below a white silk shirt. Bucks baby, you have bucks. The guy shifted, one foot then the other. Either hyper or impatient, he stepped into the side yard inspecting the grounds.

I should have moved, dammit! Shouldn't have been so nosey? Stupid! She called out his name, Norm. He turned. I stood took two steps and then walked the line of the hedge to the street. Walking swiftly, but not so to call attention? I reached the car, hearing their talk continue.

"Jan dear. Do the Flemings have a gardener?"

"No, I don't believe so. Or, at least they never said. Mr. Fleming loves keeping the yard and she concentrates lovingly on the roses. I suppose you would think a gardener does all this."

He checked the rear view after pulling away from the curb. A youngster sat on the curb, a skate board in his lap. Probably that bitch's kid, he presumed.

Son-of-a-bitch! Close, that was close. A few seconds sooner would have been disastrous. Hadn't thought of it before now? Getting caught. What would I have done?

What if she was in my grip, on the way to the bedroom. Ring! Ring! The door. Anyone interested in seeing the house wouldn't just leave. They'd want a look, having come far perhaps.

The door ajar, they'd walk in and interrupt. Don't want interruptions. No. No. No. Have to silence her without the satisfaction, without gratification. Looking on it now, that bitch and her husband came at a good time after all. If it had to happen, it was good that it did that way. I needed a reality check. Be more careful.

Feeling calmer now, he headed for Lady and the quiet of his den to re-plan.

Dan smiled as Jen slid in opposite him. "Starting my ten-minute break. That invitation still on?"

"It certainly is. Have you had a chance to eat this morning? Can I buy you a bite?."

"Thank you, but no. I take a half toast or bites of fruit or bacon on the run usually. If it's slow, I might choose to sit a minute. Like this, only most times alone. This is nice. Thank you."

"The pleasure's all mine, Jen."

Swallowing her sip, "so what brings you to our town? If I'm not imposing."

Dan shifted, creaking the old bench seat of oak. "Well I am here on business of sorts. Doing a bit of investigating for an insurance company, no big deal. Sensing her deeper curiosity he covered, "that's why I sat with your police chief in here one day, get some info."

"So you're a P.I., as they say?"

"Not really. Half Investigator, half Lawyer. On my own. Freelancer, you know. Mostly for insurance fraud cases, that type of thing." He fidgeted a bit, uncustomary for him. Shouldn't fib like this, especially to her?

Uncomfortable with it, "So, up and straight. This your hometown? Single, kids, significant other? Tell me about you, the true Jennifer."

"You in town investigating me?" He felt a bit flushed. "No, no just interested."

Feeling a bit unsettled now herself, yet somehow excited, Jen shifted in her seat, picking up the pack of Salems spinning it around on the table. "Well my family moved here when I was entering Mendelson High. I felt out of place for a while, but it was only temporary. Was a

B-student, did Drama club two years, cheerleader one year realizing I didn't fit in. Too many egos"

She sipped a mouthful. "Two months before graduation, a visit to the doctor told me that the romantic and passionate Spring night at Sculley Pond with six-month steady Jimmy Drake, proof of how fertile I am. I decided to keep the baby. Jimmy decided to continue his college plans. His plan to return each Summer changed to working at school each Summer.

He came back here several times before moving permanently. He does visit now and again, sends money and gifts for Angie."

Checking his eyes gave her a sense of an upcoming question. "No, no man in my life. There's been two or three over fifteen years. One I actually allowed to move in after we dated for eight months. We actually had a decent relationship. His name is Don, drove truck for Hale Sand and Gravel six days a week. A hard worker. He was good to Angie. She liked him."

She checked her watch. "It was nearly three years that we were together. And yes, we loved each other. I found a ring one day in the glove compartment of his pick up. It remained there for another six months. I used to check every now and then. No pressure. I kept it to myself, waiting, waiting."

"Then came the reflections of Afghanistan, where he had done two tours. The visits to the Vet Hospital in Drury began. Then the combining of beer and medications. It was downhill from there. I couldn't help. One afternoon when Angie and I came home, he was gone. Received a card two months later from Florida where he is living with his widowed Mamma. Wrote how he much loves Angie and wished us his best. That was that. And here I am." A sad smile etched her face.

Then just as quick, she brightened. She smiled broadly. More becoming her personality, accompanied with a winking-left eye. "I'm back to work. Hope's I wasn't a bore? Haven't spoken like that with anyone in a long time, and with a stranger? Dan. You're sure you're not a shrink?"

Dan was getting used to this waitress's brighter side.

Dan left his motel room early the next morning for Plymouth, about a twenty minute drive.

He seized upon the opportunity to become a tourist for a few hours, visiting Plymouth rock housed in it's caged space where tourists could look down upon it, imagining a first settler stepping and standing a moment. He happened to be thinking someone driving from Alabama or South Dakota on vacation to visit this historic site, when overhearing a fella, he assumed from the south drawling into his wife's ear. "All this way to look at a rock. Not even a pilgrim footprint on it. And why's it in a space fifteen feet deep. Afraid someone 'll chip off a piece."

Sometimes people forget it's simply the significance of the history, and not the appearance of the

Historical elements alone. In this case it may be the expectancy to see a more significant larger than life edifices, maybe a statue of Columbus or some lowly pilgrim, his or her foot set upon this majestic stone set in a salty wave. Not so.

Simply noted, here it is, a rock, supposedly the one our first pilgrim stepped upon. And that is that.

I walked the jetty stretching 400 feet into the salty brine, passing families sitting on the flat rock balancing sandwiches and drinks. Huddled groups of teens, some professing openly that they a couple, holding hands. Others puffing their first cigarette by the look. And the fishermen, young and old patiently reeling in and casting out.

That bit of exercise required some refreshment. Wandering the downtown, I came upon an inviting Bard's Pub, wherein enjoyed a draft and crab cake sandwich before heading back to Middleton.

Dan pulled into a small store in Carver just before the Middleton town line. The map bought a week ago he had misplaced. Unusual for him.

By appearance this place stood here for the past hundred and fifty years. It wasn't messy really, just old, with a porch built in the front. Like you'd see in an old western running the length of town in front of the bank, general store and saloon.

The bell ringing above the door told someone, somewhere, you were here, reminding me of the diner. "Hello, be right out," a female voice echoed from behind a half-open door in the back.

"Don't rush on my account," I answered. "Just looking for an area map."

"On the stand next to the counter where the register is," she instructed a second before her short, stout      self appeared, arms cradling a dozen or so cartons of cigarettes. Dumping them on the counter,  "people continue to smoke'em, got to sell them I suppose. Find the right map?"

"Yes, thank you. Just what I need."

"Mabel's my name. Run the store with my husband Jake. Just telling you who we are case you plan to move here. Want to make newcomers welcome." A thin smile showing, "need the business too."

"Well my name is Dan. And in fact, am looking at property in this area."

"You wouldn't be interested in operating a longstanding establishment locally would you?"a sly grin returning on her round face. "Thinking of selling out," Dan leading her on.

"I may just consider it for the right price." She sat, ample behind on the wooden stool at the counter.  "Started working in this place when I was four years old. Stocked canned goods on the bottom shelves. Been in the Curry family now for fifty years. Dad bought out old Jim Stanton in 1954. Good gods, listen to me. Sorry for babbling. Anything else?"

"Just the map thanks, Mabel. Maybe I'll be back with an offer." She snickered. "Give you a deal" .

Nice gal I thought stepping to the parking lot taking a second to look around, forgetting I had the rental. Getting old was my excuse to myself.

Hearing footsteps moments after Dan left, Mabel spoke without turning, "think of something else?"

"What was that?" Answered a surprised tone. Mabel turned now, "Oh sorry Nathan. Thought you were the guy who just left coming back for something. How you doing today? Been a stranger for a while now."

"Been okay, can't complain. That guy you speak of, he isn't from here right?"

"No. Told me he's looking into moving here though. Just stopped in to buy a map of the area. Seems pleasant. Didn't talk a whole lot"

"Well thank you Mabel." Nathan dropped a dollar on the counter for the real estate paper he slid under his arm.

Strange bird Mabel thought watching him saunter out. Made her nervous each time he stopped in. Always that grim look about his face. Eyes dark deep-set, hiding within cave openings of bone under wide brows, peeking at you when he starts talks before staring past over your shoulders, his mind finding two places at the same time.

Her mind mulled the history. She knew his parents ever since she can remember. Saw them fairly regularly before his mother died. Good folks. Mother, especially pleasant, father a bit odd. A look-a-like grimness to his son she now pieced together. Surprised she had not recognized this before.

His Mother died of breast cancer. The Father worked his small vegetable farm and did carpentry jobs. Good finish-carpenter in the opinion of most folks he did work for.

A year or so after Mildred died he took up with Marie Patterson a local real estate agent. The match-up seemed at odds to most everyone. Jimbo, as the father was known, had unruly hair. Clean shaven once a week, and wore the same clothes for days in a row. That changed when Millie happened along. Grim frown lines turned reversed, smiled occasionally.

A little action hardened him a bit, no pun intended, but seemed also to have softened him. Rumored he was infatuated with her. Consumed even, some say. Worst of it being that Nathan was left out. Pushed away really in the wake of their relationship. They may have married? If so must have been private. She stayed at the homestead like it was a motel, still maintaining her own home.

Marie somehow convinced Jimbo into dividing the ten acres, suitable for a four-house lot sub-division surrounded by wetland preserve. Plans were thwarted though with the environmental people, local as well as State stepping in and declaring it all wetlands. Marie still made out selling it in entirety to the town for $800.000.00. The town now had a new wildlife preserve. Nathan, left with the house and 1 acre.

Next thing you know Marie sold out, moved to Florida. I forget where. Near St. Augustine I believe where she opened an office. She was a hard headed woman. Though not hard enough. Story filtering back here telling that she went out on her new love interest's boat, slipped hitting her head on the bow rail and fell overboard. By the time someone missed her, she was doing the dead-woman's float. What goes around comes, . . . Mabel thought privately, cashing out the register. Time to close.

With Joe's authorized letter of introduction Dan visited Chiefs of police in Carver, Halifax, Plymouth, Carver, Plympton, the three Bridgewaters, and Lakeville. These towns closest to surrounding Mendelson. It was worth a shot.

Of those individuals known to local authorities having records of sexual assault on down to exposure, five had moved away and two had died. The remainder didn't even come close to the profile, or from Dan's experience, the brains to plan and maneuver like this cozy killer. The person could live a distance away perhaps. Though no murders of this type had occurred, at least not within a year near here, leaving Dan the thought of a nut case with roots here.

A loner, living in a world of his or her own. Quiet, cunning, shy, living a fantasy. He would begin by scouring the country side, the back roads, where such people often hide.

# Chapter Seven

Jan fingered the key pad. At the click she keyed the lock and let herself in. Sniffing the air a bit musty, she opened a few windows and edged open the patio slider.

The Laceys closed up the house a week ago spending two weeks on the Vineyard. "Where I should be," Jan muttered openly, immediately answering herself. "Yeah right," aware of the four to six thousand a week being the cost of rentals there.

Someday she thought, smiling to herself and giving the kitchen and rest of the downstairs a final walk through to be sure ready for the scrutiny of home seekers.

Binoculars pulled her closer. More beautiful and sexier than ever. He slowly turned the focus, studying her skirt rising up thighs. He could taste her skin. Her frame arched, opening the drapes to light the den with sunlight. Aroused, his head fell back, eyes closing. Control, control. Stay in control he pleaded with himself. The time for that will come. He crept closer. He smelled her sweetness, the fresh smell of Spring imbedded in her pores.

Dan happened upon a dirt road aligned by Cranberry bogs, a good section between stretches of woods. He imagined deer plentiful here in this New England terrain. He drove through the narrow space made by one gate left open.

If found trespassing, or happened upon by the owner, he would either get thrown off the property, or be a  welcomed visitor. Not that he was in the mood to visit.

A small white clapboard house lay ahead secluded, No signs of a farm operation. A small barn, separate two-car-garage.  He stopped in front, pressed on the horn twice. No signs of life. A bark came from inside seconds before the dog's head parted the curtains, chin settling on the sill.

Dan got out, spinning around every several steps scanning the premises momentarily, before returning to the car making a mental note to revisit.

Across town Nathan suppressed desires, moving to the cover of a front hedge some six feet high. Kneeling a few minutes to listen and study the surroundings again, he moved to the slider. Another moment and he entered through the opening, met with the beat of light jazz and Jan humming while her light foot steps descended from upstairs.

His heart began to race. He opened and closed both fists, flexing fingers. Her short heels clicked onto dining room hardwood. She was coming his way. Moving slightly to relieve body tension, he rose off one knee into a low crouch just inside the kitchen archway.

Jan stepped by the dining table five feet from him stopping suddenly. She poked her head in front of the small wall mirror. Deciding to refresh her lipstick she turned reaching into her bag on the table, back to the mirror. Hearing her speak to the mirror, eyes concentrating on painting her lips, came his opportune moment.

A hand suddenly appeared in the mirror, a soft pink line of lipstick trailed across her cheek. Stunned, she instinctively arched backward and turned, feeling release. Spinning onto one knee, she was nearly up when his hand grasped her ankle jerking her down hard, arms extending back as her head smashed against the hard oak boards. Her body relaxed into a rag-doll.

He felt her pulse. "No, no. Dammit, no! We're just beginning." He held the sides of his head.

Sweat dripped down his nose. What to do. Calming himself. "My precious, this cannot be."

He stood studying the room. Nothing broken, just a bit disturbed. He stood the chair, straightened the small area rug, and wiped the floor with a dish-towel before placing against her cut.

Moving quickly, he lifted placing her at the patio doors. He walked swiftly to his car retrieving an old Army blanket from the trunk.

Moments after re-surveying the dining room and kitchen, he was out and placing her body in the trunk.

Dropping the tire jack he had set up earlier telling any nosey neighbors it was simply some poor devil with a flat .

The tall hedge provided adequate cover. Some chance involved, but luck with him so far. This unplanned turn of events somehow increased his excitement. In nervous anticipation he chewed a fingernail wiping chin drool with his sleeve and driving away.


Janine Shepard had vanished three weeks ago. No witnesses, no clues. Exception being, and not really a clue, learning that she had called from this home on a prior Sunday reporting suspicious activity. That report holding no lead.

Each home and the occupants had been painstakingly sought and interviewed. Her closest friends and out of state relatives offered suggestions at our pleading. That this behavior so unbecoming of her, none made sense. She wouldn't have left for a destination, or to visit without taking personal belongings or telling anyone. No one held a clue. She lived alone, and aside from her part-time office secretary, worked basically alone.

She had scheduled the open house that Sunday. She had arrived, for her car was in the driveway. No signs of a struggle. Nothing in the house missing. Only finger prints found were family members, Janine's, a friend of the daughter, and a Fed-Ex delivery person from Saturday who had opened the screen door for access to the front door's brass knocker.

Being on a Sunday, the traffic on the street was reduced. Including mail carriers, delivery people, florists. Telephone workers, oil delivery, cleaners, etc.

Two teens remembered a car on the sidewalk nearer the neighbors hedge. But didn't know the model or even looked at the plate. It might have been gray, and real clean.

Janine's planner had only this open house penned in. And to call her sister. That didn't happen. Everything was cold. Ice cold like the others. This the common item, no evidence. Was our suspicion of a serial killer, now turned kidnapper? Stealing her away. To savor another time perhaps?

Dan remained in town for two weeks. He continued calling Joe once a week, traveling back twice a month just to have a peek around, as he puts it. What was becoming obviously a need to see Jen? Their relationship indeed advancing to a serious side, though neither considering it a long term. Yet.

Dan picked up on a note scribbled in his pad seven months before. 'That arm-house. Old. Secluded.'

An hour later he pushed the old wooden gate aside. The NO TRESPASSING-POLICE TAKE NOTICE SIGNS having fallen from the last rusty nail holding them.

He drove the narrow drive, weeds overgrown on either side slapping the car, smaller tree branches sounding chalk on a blackboard.

He remembered what Chief Joe had said. Same family owning the property for years. They died, son Nathan had moved, returning for his mother's funeral. Still around, but seldom seen. Rumored he was miffed with the relationship his father had been involved in after Mother died. Never a problem though to police, or anyone around town.

Two hundred yards form the house, Dan parked the car. The place now appearing deserted. An old rusted pick-up sat under an old Elm. A tractor, apparently sitting for many years nearly engulfed in weeds. Starting the engine and pulling closer surprised a racoon scurrying from under the front porch.  The old barn doors were closed. The windows of the house had no curtains. Three windows on the second floor and two on the first floor were broken. A couple old trash barrels stood on end near the stairs. Several empty beer cans and a Jack Daniel's empty littered nearby. Evidence perhaps of teens partying.

I stood stationary, silent listening, eyes scanning. So as not to surprise another trespasser I hollered loudly. The silence continuing. All I'd need is to alarm the owner or anyone who may be armed. Or perhaps teens having a first sexual or drug experience in the barn. That thought led me to open the barn door. Aside from a couple pigeons cooing, nothing moved. It smelled only of dry hay in the heat of day.

Strolling to the house I knocked first on the peeling front door. Then a window sash. A look through the broken window found bare floors, walls, and no kitchen furniture. Or appliances.

"Well, why not", convincing myself.. I'm here. Might as well poke around. About to push on the door, I held back entering, opting to circle the outside first.

The back was much the same. More broken windows and litter. I knocked once before pushing the rear door open enough to slip in. Stale hot air from the August sun baking the roof . The only air coming from an occasional breeze through broken panes.

Old newspapers sat spread in one corner under an old moldy dog dish. Wallpaper in spots drooped off dried paste. Aside from an old maple end table and empty socket, no shade lamp, no furniture remained.  Only the indents on the wide oak flooring left from what furniture was here.

Every other stair tread creaked while stepping upstairs. I speculated, a result from kids double-hopping as they grew older, as I once did. The rail was dust covered, no signs of hands holding on recently.

At the top sat empty bedrooms and a full bath. An area rug laid outside each bedroom. The toilet water un-flushed and rusty. The tub and sink un-scrubbed. Vandals apparently afraid to enter these rooms with no evidence of hand or footprints in all the dust.

Having had enough, I stepped out again, to the back yard. Hoping for a breeze, I headed for the shade of a friendly old oak. A smell gathered at my nose. . .sweet,. . . no, flowery . . .or is it more like baby powder?  What is it? I looked for a flowering shrub, a flower bed, plants, discovering none.

Walking no more than ten paces, the smell was gone. Maybe honeysuckle, a turnabout seeing none.  A few minutes of shade and brow-wiping, I strolled slowly while dialing the Chief., curious how long this place vacant, and whether Joe knew the recent history?  Beth answered her pleasant hello before hitting transfer.

"Hi Dan. Beth tells me you have questions regarding the old farm. No. Haven't been around that place for a while?  Driven by. Never any reason to go onto the property in years. Not since they passed away. Thought the son, Nathan might still be there. Though he could have moved on. We could check with town hall Assessors office if you want to?"

"Totally abandoned you say. I'm a bit surprised I guess. Kid still had a few acres and the home. That run down huh?  Well maybe he left and is going to sell. No for sale signs?  Well let's check records then tomorrow. Offices closed at this hour. Coincidence your calling.  I've worked out a plan. Stop in why don't you so we can discuss it before I select a couple of my people and lay it out."

"What do you mean, plan, Joe?" "Stop in, you'll see. Want to keep it hush."

Joe was bent over his desk when Dan arrived. "Hi Dan. You didn't have to rush in."

"Well! You piqued my interest with this plan of yours."

"What do you think of this? You, me, Detective Paulson, and maybe one more. I don't want to include too many on this. Actually it depends on the number of open-houses locally. Even thought maybe involving Carver, Halifax or Plymouth."

"I digress. We select three or four open houses and a set-up a watch. You, me, Paulson, and whoever else, gets dropped off the night before, staying within the home. The owners leave the next day so the realtor can do her thing."

"Had entertained the thought you might know of a female agent, or using my female officer Kara Trent, to act as the realtor. She'd be disguised with blonde wig and dressed business-like. Thinking more on it, decided if we're on the site the actual realtor could remain. If, as I suspect, this nut-ball pre-selects his prey, in their thirties, and attractive. Thoughts thus far?"

"I think it's worth a shot, Joe. Although being awhile since the last killing, might be a waste of time and manpower. Though nothing ventured, nothing gained. When you're ready, let me know my assignment." Dan knew what Joe was dealing with and considered this would help him personally as well.

Joe sat edged partly on the table. " Well I have to speak to a couple Realtors. See how they take to

acting like ponds in our little chess game."

And so the plan moved forward Two weeks later, Dan sat in the basement of 22 Pondview Terrace, a new home in a half complete development in south Mendelson.

Joe sat in a basement of an older home on Smith Ave. Detective Jim Paulson in North Mendelson on Acorn Drive. Each of these purposely advertised as noon-time openings, not leaving the agent compromised. They would each then move to a second scheduled location. One in Mendelson, two in Carver.

Halifax Chief Wilson was stationed at an open house in his town, and Chief Clooney at a location in his town of Rochester.

This routine carried on for three week-ends within a five-town area with nothing even slightly suspicious resulting. Joe Broderick had always been strong willed. Determined in his work ethic.

Yeah, he had experienced bitterness before, some sadness, blues moments perhaps from which he quickly fortified his mind, and recovered. Viewing a child's lifeless body, a teen female driver's beautiful blonde hair matted in blood sticking to the windshield afg6er taking her final breath. But he dealt with it and though bothered for a time, moved on. Now though he was experiencing a different side.

Sensing this preying Joe's mind, Dan and others spoke to him at various times hoping to ease his frustration.

Joe fronted his best face, nodded his usual compliant "no problem" response, concealing inside the slow burn, fed by the fuel of failure.

# Chapter Eight

Nathan stood naked, eyes gathering-in every inch of his prize as she slept. Mama's medicine calmed her. He hung her skirt and blouse on a hanger. Neatly folded her bra and panties before covering her with the sheet earlier. The same sheet he now pulled down ever so slowly exposing one breast, then the other. So smooth, milky white. Skin unblemished, sculptured tight to her bones, her chin her neck. He placed his hand over her heart feeling the rhythmic beat. Bending forward his ear picked up the beat.

"My precious Marie." His lips pursed her nipple, tongue slowly circling the detail. His left hand slid down, fingers pausing, combing down her silky patch. Straightening his middle finger, he pressed in making tiny circles.

He pushed his throbbing hardness against the side board. Parting her thighs slightly, he licked his lips. "Not yet, my sweet. Mamma? You'd like her too, wouldn't you? Do you like this room Mamma? I had to rearrange everything here. It was a lot of work."

A pretty and petite thirty something stood smiling when Dan closed the door behind him to the Tax Collector's office before stepping forward and positioning folded arms on the counter top.

"Good morning. How can I help you sir?"

Dan, keen on addressing people by name whenever possible, had gathered hers from the name plate on her desk. "Well Miss Bradshaw my name is Dan Hudson. Your police chief is familiar with my work completing investigations for various insurance companies. At the moment I am interested in knowing the status of the property at 1510 Plymouth Street. Whether it recently changed hands, who pays the taxes, that sort of info. That's about it. I'd appreciate what info you have."

After jotting down the address on her pad, "one moment Mr. . .Hudson you said, right?"

Standing at her desk back to Dan, she dialed her phone. "Hi Chief, sorry to bother you. A Dan Hudson is here. Says you know him? Sure thing Chief, and thank you."

Turning, "be back in a jiff, Mr. Hudson. Smiling, "the Chief says hi." Dan smiled back. "Always best to be sure of things, right Susan?"

Susan stooped pulling open a low file drawer. A few strokes of her pen and she returned to the counter. She re-wrote the info on an index card before turning it. Turning it she used her pencil as a pointer.

"Well Dan, here is the name of the listed owner and tax-payer to whom bills are sent. This is the assessed value and the estimated market value of the house, the barn, sheds and the land. Last change was after Jimbo passed, leaving son Nathan, Nathan Bass that is. Mr. Bass was known locally and familiarly as Jimbo, she chuckled."

Dan's investigatory senses kicked in. "So Sue, Nathan has paid the taxes since?"

"That's right. Well, that is the bill has been paid, and on time. Assuming it mailed to Nathan, that he pays it. Although someone else could pay. I'm being too technical"

"I get what you intend, Sue. You know this Nathan?"

"Not really. Know what he looks like. Never acquainted though. According to town records payment is made by mail. For some reason we record if paid here at the office or by mail. Haven't seen him myself for a long time."

"Okay Sue, thanks for this. Reason for asking. I was over by the place and it looks abandoned." Handing her his card, "I'd appreciate your calling should you hear anything. About the property or him. You know, like if he moved away or whatever."

"Sure enough." She smiled, shaking Dan's extended hand.

Not much info there he contended, skipping down granite steps. Checking the time, he continued across Mechanic Street onto Main hoping Jen was on her lunch break.

Pausing at the window, he placed his face and nose against it, waiting. She turned, seeing his nose flattened. She stopped hands on hips grinning broadly before pointing to at the side of her head. A hand in a rotating motion. He went in. "We concur," the cook and other waitress told him.

"Well I do try and get a smile out of some people. No one here appreciating it." The waitress winked, " I don't believe it's we you did it for."

He took the end seat at the counter. "Hi big boy. Looking for anyone special?", Jen teasingly whispered in a throaty tone.

"Dan leaned forward, "Yeah. A girl works here. A sweet thing. Pretty, nice eyes, a slender, nice butt."

"She sounds familiar, but she's seeing someone. Although if you're really interested". . .Dan interrupted, touching her hand. "Thought you might be taking a break.  Share a bite."

"Jen turned the other waitress, "Carol, do you, . . . Carol, taking an order, broke her off, hand gesturing approval.

Jen wrote down her and Dan's order placing it on the spin wheel at the open divider to the kitchen. She then propped herself on the stool next to Dan, leaning to kiss his cheek. He did the same. They talked, ate, held hands.


On the way home Dan picked up a Pinot Noir they would share later. He was getting into his car when the Chief's car pulled aside. The window came down.

" Anything at the Collector's office of any use Dan?" Dan leaned out his window. Nah, not really.  Kid, Nathan still pays the taxes. Property still listed in his name. Like I said earlier, it appears abandoned. Maybe we should check it now and again. Ask around if anyone has seen him or anyone aware if he moved. Never know."

"I'll have my officers keep a heads up. Check the property now and then. If for no other reason, check teen action up there." His radio squawked. "Got to go Dan. Quickly turning back, " Bet I can guess where your off to," spying the wine Dan held, revved the engine with a wink and a grin.

The combo of a Heineken and the comfort of the sofa cushions had Dan drifting off during the sixth inning of the college world series Texas-UCLA match-up. Awake to see the final batter, he pressed the off button. Is that the shower running?  Jen?

Standing in the hall, head arched upward, the bathroom door opened slightly. "Hey sleepy head, want to wash my back?"

"Isn't Angie due home?" Jen struck a pose, leg raised, foot resting on the edge of the tub. "Her friend Megan invited her to stay for dinner. Plenty of time."

Dan's dock siders landed on the first stair, two more stairs shirt off, at the landing pants off, boxers fell on the tiled bath. Jen slid the curtain aside again holding the soap between her breasts in another provocative pose. "Suds me up big guy? " Dan's left foot was in the shower. A pause . . ."Dammit. Give me a second."

Hearing the hardy stream, "Couldn't you have been better prepared?"

A minute later she welcomed him in. Both hungry with passion, making love till the water cool and he carried Jen laying her on the bed. An hour later dressed in robes, they sipped wine, dipped warm bread in olive oil before enjoying  pasta and butter, sprinkled with Parmesan.

" Jen, are you familiar with a Nathan Bass? Owns the old family homestead way out on Plymouth Street."

She squinted, her eyes self-examining in thought.  "Yeah. He comes in now and again. Mostly for take-out. Around supper time. Once in awhile has breakfast at the counter. Not a talker. Hi, good morning, thank you. Come to think of it hasn't been in for a while. Quite awhile."

Dan used his napkin. "That answered my next question. Trying to find out when and if he's gone. The property certainly shows that, lying vacant and un-lived in for some time. Any friends, relatives?"

Jen finished chewing her last bit. "Can't say? Always alone at the café. After high school he moved away at some point. You heard the story right?  About his mother's illness and sometime after his father taking up with Emily Patterson. Nathan apparently didn't approve or didn't like her, whatever. You know the rest. Remember you saying someone told you."

"Strange, he'd move from a place he owns outright. Letting it rundown the way it is. I don't want to create a stir, but think I'll check with a couple closer neighbors to the property.  Though the closest as I recall is a couple thousand feet. Oh well. Let's get to more important things," nuzzling her neck.

"Doesn't your testosterone tank ever register on low?" Dan looked in her eyes. "Not with someone special. I never tire of our love-making. Just holding you."

Jen sighed, cuddling up. "Me too."

Janine's lids blinked open greeting light filtering in and out. Like a blind opening and closing. Her nostrils collected a dankness. Semi-conscience, she tried lifting her head, eyes squinting made her forehead hurt. She went to move her arm to feel why but could not, feeling restrained somehow.

She felt the urge to lick her lips, to swallow, lips frozen together and stretched, held tight, and only able to breathe through her nose. She inhaled a strange smell. Something cooking perhaps, and dirt?

Whatever it was aroused her. Looking down inspecting herself her eyes saw grey duct tape tight on her mouth, hands tied to at her sides with thin clothesline rope. Feet with no shoes, bound together with tape. Turning her head toward a bubbling sound she spotted a stove A pot, the source of the noise, steams rising.

The walls were of flat stone like those of an old cellar. Her heart pounded now. She closed her eyes as her mind ran a marathon spinning with thought and questions, and horror. Panicking, unable to put it down nor spit it out, a blanket of sweat covering her head and neck, running her chest.. She arched her body side to side.

"Easy, easy now," a soft-spoken tone. "Didn't know you awake?" Seeing her eyes in panic, he ripped away the tape leaving blood speckles where the tape lifted the skin.

Janine gave a painful moan, turned her head down spitting bile onto the sheet.

"Sorry my sweet." He quickly went to the sink filling a small basin setting it on the night stand.

What is this nightmare?! Body rigid, muscles taut, Jan trembled uncontrollably.

Wetting the cloth, he leaned to her. Jan flinched. "What are you doing? What is happening? Tears welled in her eyes, fear darting wide pupils' side to side video taping her surroundings, mind fraught with terror, trying to quickly make sense.

"Calm yourself sweet Marie, . . . I mean, Janine. He pressed one hand gently, but firmly on her shoulder, the other softly wiping her forehead, mouth and neck.

Jan's heart pounding eased a bit. Her body moved up and down, swayed right and left wrists and legs pulling on tape and rope. She started to gag on bile entering her throat. Her tongue and mouth so dry she unable to back it down. Choking, she turned away again coughing up liquid on the sheet.

He held her shoulders forcing her down, hushing her with surprising gentleness. His finger went quickly in and out of her mouth. Something stuck beneath her tongue. She tried freeing it, moving it with her tongue, but it was gone.

Her eye lids grew heavy, closing. What is this?. . . Who is this? The soreness as he touched her forehead. The mirror! . . .Falling!. . .My God, I'm his captive. Her mind raced with panic, yet her body remaining calm.

He placed the cloth in the basin. Walking to the foot of the bed he loosened the sheet pulling it up, holding her in the air as he slid it under and off. He returned to the basin ringing out the cloth before tossing it into a rubbish basket, and emptying the basin into the sink.

Refilling it with fresh water and getting a clean cloth, he wiped it over her forehead and face. After rinsing, methodically moved the cloth over her chest and under each breast down her stomach and pelvic area, thighs and legs. He turned her over gently,,completing his task.

She ceased attempting to move, hearing light jazz with piano playing in the background. Why so calm she wondered, the last bit of pill dissolving in her mouth.

His voice. What is he saying?

"Welcome my dearest.". . .Brushing his lips along the side of her supple breast. "Sleep well while I prepare our feast. You must be famished."

Dan picked up the apartment after Jen left for the diner. He was going to get up and eat breakfast with her, but eyeing the hands sitting at five-thirty opted to sleep in. Minutes later it seemed, he felt her lips against his cheek, "see you later sleepy-head."

An hour later he made coffee, cooked an egg and watched twenty minutes of the Today show before deciding a ride in the country was in order.

" My aging bladder doesn't hold what it used to. Damn it!" An urge to piss forcing Dan to pull into the old ruts of a tractor trail edged with aging Oaks and overgrown raspberry bushes. Standing next to the car he washed his tire scolding himself for knowing better than drinking three cups of coffee..

And how embarrassing if someone hap-by.

Finished, he quickly pulled away driving slowly further down Plymouth slowing at what the mail box identified as number 1502. He pulled into the driveway. Clothes hung on the line in the side yard. "Don't see that much anymore," he whispered into the air.

His second knock on the wooden screen door cautioned a shadow peeking down the hallway.

"Who's knocking?"

Positioning myself to be in full view through the screen door. "Sorry to bother you. My name is Dan Hudson. I'm an insurance investigator. Know your Chief Broderick."

Footsteps scuffled closer. "Just wanted to ask a couple questions about your neighbor's property." She looked to be in her eighties, if a day. Dressed in slippers and a house coat. Wearing white socks below high-water pajamas.

"You mean the Bass' place? They selling?  Or should say, the boy selling?"

She came through the door onto the porch, heading for one of the two ratan chairs.

"Take a chair. Don't want to answer anything personal you know!" Suddenly appearing like she just realized what she had on, fingers brushing her hair back. "Gee I must look,. . .excuse my appearance. Made breakfast, put two loads in the washer, baked some raisin cookies. Didn't count on some-one coming by?  I suppose one should always prepare."

"I the one should be apologizing. Just popping in like this." He settled back taking this all in a moment. It reminded him, as did she, of growing up in the mid-west. Same likeness of surroundings. Farm house and barn, fields, clothes on the line. Granny on the porch.

Another reminder that across the country there  remnants of sameness. Residential and suburban. Main streets, highways and bi-ways. Diners, down towns and malls. Pizza Huts and Burger Kings. People working, talking the news, families laughing one day, feuding momentarily the next. And grandmothers baking cookies.

Her head came forward, her stare bringing me back. Grinning, "sorry. Just wondering about that place," pointing. "Stopped by there the other day. Appears deserted, rundown. Several windows are broken, litter about the yard. Peeked in a window or two, No furniture. Ever see or hear anyone over there?  Know if he moved on?"

She still stared, eyes questioning, while the nail on her forefinger tapped against a front tooth.

Pre-empting her asking,  "Reason is, I have some concern about a place like that becoming a fire hazard. Or vandals and homeless people moving in causing a possible liability risk."

Her tiny shoulders relaxed. "Why if a fire went unnoticed, it could spread to our land. Have heard those um, four wheelers are they, romping out back. Anyway, haven't seen Nathan in I don't recall when. Months, it must be. Course I don't get about like I used to. Pa's gone, three years this November. My son, Hank lives with me. Moved back after his divorce. Cares for the place. Feeds the one cow and takes care of two horses. He likes to ride. Plants a vegetable garden in Summer. Not a real farm any longer."

She rose a second to bring her chair closer. "Don't hear like I used to. And don't like speaking loud. Was at a wedding reception at the Legion last week? A DJ played so loud I couldn't enjoy speaking with those at our table until he took a break or played a slow one."

Dan stifled a yawn before biting his lip, maintaining his usual patience with older folk.

"Anyway my son takes the commuter train to Boston. Works for a accounting firm there. My daughter lives in Carver, just twenty minutes really. She'll pick up my grandson from school and drive here for a visit. Mostly every Wednesday. A Sunday maybe once a month. And in turn, Hank and I are invited there once a month for Sunday dinner. Listen to me the babbler. I don't think Hank will know much more. He takes walks along that area with his Golden Retriever. Other than that sticks pretty much to home and goes into town to shop or share a couple beers with his pals at the Elk's lodge. You know Nathan used to attend the Congregational church  after his parents passed. Can't say as I've seen him attending for some time?  That Nathan works at a hospital, I believe. Or maybe a nursing home or clinic. Dresses in those green duds, you know, like they wear."

Dan stood. "Well I don't want to take any more of your day. I do appreciate your taking the time. Enjoyed our visit."

She took Dan's hand at the offer to help her up. "I'll tell Hank to keep an eye out."

"Good idea. Thank you again".

I opened the car door, turning back hearing her raised voice. "That Nathan had a truck and a nice car. Real fancy. You know a few weeks ago I couldn't sleep. Got up to read a little while. Don't normally have a car go by at three-thirty in the morning? So when I heard it I glanced out. Was a full moon? It was a car like his I think. Probably nothing to it! Bye now."

I nodded and waved. Three thirty in the morning? Maybe he swung by to check on the property on the way from a late night out. Why the concern though? The way he's let it go down. Listen to me! Could have been anyone out late, or driving into work early?.

Dan went the opposite way slowing at a newer garrison a thousand feet or so after the Bass place. Deciding to turn in. He estimated the house ten or so years' old. What the chances they even know Nathan or the Bass name for that matter. No cars, and no answer of the bell, he headed for the diner and the meatloaf Wednesday special.

Nathan pulled his Dockers from the dryer giving them a shake and pulled them on. He tossed the flannel shirt aside opting for the hundred percent cotton. Ironing it didn't bother him. Mother taught him to use an iron well, creasing pants and shirts properly. "In case you decide on college or live on your own," she'd say.

Dressed, he stepped into dock-siders after one last check n the mirror, running his hand over his chin, pressing his hair down, and clenching his teeth, stretching upper and lower lips in examination. After splashing on a little Old Spice Red Zone,he headed to the kitchen. Well, kitchen, dining room and sitting area combined. His new quarters open-spaced, except for the bedrooms.

He lifted the cover on the larger pot turning down the burner before replacing the lid only partially allowing steam to escape before pulling the oven door a smidgeon checking the chicken.

"Almost," announcing aloud. He reached for the foiled wrapper holding the Italian bread. Removing it he placed it on the bread board. Lifting the wide knife from the draw he cut one inch slices arranging them on a plate, and setting it on the table.

He checked the table again. Salad bowls, dinner plates, water and wine glasses, butter, Parmesan, olive oil for dipping, white cloth napkins, place settings.

He removed the chicken from the oven carving small pieces into a bowl. Emptying the pot of pasta into the caldron to drain, he spread it into a white serving dish, and then placed chicken pieces one by one over the pasta before placing it on the table next to the tomato sauce boat. The same one Mamma filled with gravy at Thanksgiving. He turned the corkscrew setting the wine to breathe.

"Time to wake my precious girl, hand touching her cheek. "I know your awake sweet thing. Saw you moving ten minutes ago and peeking about. Dinner smells good? I've prepared this especially for you. Come now."

He untied her wrists, leaving her ankles taped, helping her to sit up. Reaching to the wardrobe dresser he removed a black dress which he gathered up placing it over her head and shoulders. The dresser table held the white string of pearls which he clasped about her neck. Lifting a brush he softly brushed her hair back.

"Don't be sad, my Darling. He bent over, placing his arms under, lifting her into a chair at the table. "Oh, how thoughtless! Do you need the bathroom ,my dearest? Can you last through dinner?"

Jan's body trembled slightly. Tears streaming her cheeks. Her head answered up and down.

"My darling, look. A wonderful meal. He struck a match lighting two tall candles. "I thought you would be delighted. What do you think?"

She forced a nod of approval. "See now, this isn't so bad. Nice really. You'll see." He placed a napkin on her lap and pushed her chair in.

Something inside him saw her differently. He studied her. She's sweet and pretty. Cute too. He was not sexually aroused. This an odd sensation!

He poured a small amount of wine into her glass and handed it to her. "Try this."

He poured into his, then reaching to tap her glass.

"To us, Dearest." He took a long sip then a mouthful prompting with the motion of his glass that she does the same. Hoping not to throw it up she placed the rim to her lips splashing a sip. A forced smile, "not bad," she managed. A voice inside speaking. He's in control. Work with him. She realized something else. Calmness somehow.

Nathan gathered salad with the tongs lifting it to her plate, then his. Sitting now, he lifted his fork. "Hope you enjoy the dressing. It's extra virgin olive oil with a touch of garlic butter. Homemade."

She actually enjoyed a few bites. Then her stomach filled with restless butterflies. She forced another bite. Then another. His eyes followed her as she set the salad fork down. "Is it the dressing?"

"No, it's good. Just not an appetite."

"We'll hold off a moment then before serving the pasta. I know you'll enjoy Mamma's, . . . face showing red. . . . "I mean, my sauce. And the bread is from a great local bakery."

Janine's mouth curved slightly. It seemed to satisfy him. Good, she thought, glancing about while he occupied capturing a cherry tomato from his salad.

"Is this a cellar?" She posed.

His fork hit his plate, forehead lining, cheeks flushed, words edgy. "Are you going to spoil this moment with questions?" Raising his napkin to his mouth, he took in a long, self-controlling breath. "There now, sweet one, ready for pasta? At least a little then."

She tried short breaths to conceal her shakiness. "Sure. It does look really good  Should I call you by name"

His fingers clenching into fists on the table. Jaw firm, teeth clamping, a forehead lined. In a flash all relaxed, forehead smooth again.

"That won't be necessary. Although you might consider an affectionate term, as you like," a wide grin spreading, making her angry inside.

She ignored it hoping he wouldn't get angry. He allowed it to pass, rising to clear the salad plates.

Returning to the table he spooned angel hair onto her plate. Lifting the oil, "just a bit of oil and garlic mix." Lifting a grater, "some fresh Parmesan." He breathed in, "smell that! Mmm . . . can't beat it. Try some my darling."

She lifted the fork, her free hand pressing on the dinner knife. If only she knew where they were. A way out.  She sniffed her fork full, "mmm is right," placing it in her mouth, chewing enthusiastically swallowing it three times. "Delicious."

His chest grew, teeth flashing a satisfied grin. "This is wonderful."

He sat down gorging mouthful after mouthful, stopping only to gulp wine, exhilaration accentuating his appetite. "Wait till you see dessert!" He smiled.

Her stomach jumped at the thought of more food, eyes moving around again taking in the surroundings. She must prepare, pleading with her dinner friend. Gods help!

Dan's eyes were bigger than his stomach. Unable to clean his plate, lost in thought, his fork twisted in the mound of mashed potato.

Jen's touch revived him. "Where are you?"

Placing the fork down.  "Thinking too much maybe. Trying to piece things together without the benefit of enough information. A waste of time really. I should know better. Learned a long time ago that you need sufficient amounts of relevant information before adequately trying to piece together a puzzle. At a dead-end. Got to broaden the scope."

Gesturing consolation, Jen fingered the back of his neck. "I can understand that. So time for a break. Drive us home."

Nathan dried the last dish placing in the cabinet. Turning he studied her laying motionless.  His emotion had worked up through dinner, lapsing now and then as she coping, to please, yet her eyes dismissive. He continued staring as he smoked the last of a joint unfinished from yesterday, exhaling into the same wall vent used for the stove hood. It is late, dark outside. It would go unnoticed.

He drank the last of his wine. His hand closed around his hardness. Feeling warm, removing his shirt, walking to the bed. He unbuckled his belt, unzipped and let his pants slide, stepping from them leaning pressing his himself against the mattress.

He lowered the sheet exposing her breasts. One hand squeezed himself releasing a slow pleasurable moan while fingers of his left hand gently played with one nipple then moving to the other. His eyes widened seeing her nipples hardening to his touch. Feeling this, his mind became riveted with expectation.

Overjoyed, he dropped his underwear lifting one leg onto the bed bringing his exposure dangling for her to see. "Open your eyes. My darling sweet girl."

Janine's eye lids remained still. "My darling wake and see. Feel me, hold me. Spread yourself. Guide me in." He felt the ooze at his tip. No, not yet. His fingers let go of her. He whispered in her ear. "Come on Baby! Ooh Baby. . . .Come to me, sweet Marie."

He stood back a step, his hardness throbbing, eager. "You bitch! This is how it is. I invite you to my home. Slave over a fine dinner. Treat you like a princess. And this is my reward!

Silence.

"Am I unworthy? Is that it? You are too good for the likes of me?

He jumped to her side on the bed stroking himself dripping a bit between her breasts before squeezing to stop further release. His hand grasped her blonde hair jerking her head forward. Her lips at his tip.

"See how shiny. Suck me, Bitch!" He brushed her lips moving it back and forth. Out of control now he daubed his release about her face. His head rose up toward the ceiling in ecstasy.

Suddenly his spine went rigid, shoulders arched back, arms flailed outward momentarily before instinctively responding to the pain at his groin. Pain abruptly turning his stomach. He screamed even louder witnessing his hands filling with blood. A section of the tip and foreskin hung spurting red over her chest.

He fell to the floor landing on his back, hands fastened to his groin. His mind elevated to frenzy. He  rolled side to side, mind racing, fighting to remain conscious.  What to do?

Janine arched upward to loosen the rope on her left wrist with the hand he had cut free. The same hand he meant for her to hold him, fondle him. She spit the saliva holding the dissolved pill meant to relax her, and with it a rubber like the piece of penis. No time to heave her guts, she force-swallowed the vomit rising in her esophagus.

Yanking the rope repeatedly the flesh tore from her wrist when it broke free. Speaking to her newly discovered inner-source. "Help me, give me your strength, stay with me!"

She rolled from the bed reaching at the tape around her ankles, shaky hands making it difficult. She wanted to look, see if he still rolled about the floor, but forced concentration on the tape.

Free she bent over staying low crawling to where the bed ended. Peeking she could see his stocking feet, heels moving scraping in pain back and forth over the floor. Throws of pain elevating in the air. Strained hoarseness, "oh gods, oh my god."

Jan's body shook, heart pounding, legs weak. She struggled a run at the one doorway being met by a wall of darkness on the other side. She knelt breathless, feeling a trace of vomit sting her dry throat. She opened her eyes wider, searching the darkness, waiting for her pupils to adjust. She rose . Stepping forward, using her arms and legs stretching and kicking feet forward. Three more steps and her outstretched hands met flat edged stone. The cellars wall, she guessed, wincing with pain and gritting her teeth to suppress her cry.

Just for the sake to keep moving she opted left, hands moving feverishly along  the stone in and out of crevasses. Is this wood?  Edge of a door?  Then the outline of a panel. A door panel. She moved her hand up and down for a knob. No knob?  She reached high feeling a metal plate, then a bolt latch. Her finger and thumb grabbled turning it a bit and it slid down. She was crying now uncontrollably, hopeful yet fearful. She wanted to stop, to listen for him, but panic stayed her quest.

The door creaked ajar just when a beam of light created the dark shadow looming across the stone as he lunged, the heavy metal flashlight crashing between her shoulder blades dropping her to her knees. Head creasing the jam. Dizzy, she picked herself up, brushing ooze from her forehead.

"You bitch! No-good bitches. A sweet girl you could have been. There is no escape. That but an old doorway from years ago. Hah, hah." She cried inward. "Dear friend, are you with me?  Vision blurring, "don't let me faint!

The light beam moved side to side, his hand uncontrolled from pain. Sights of him partially lit up. He was covered in blood, one hand at his crotch holding duct tape used to secure the wound. His face wild, a grotesqueness flashing on the screen of a monster thriller movie. Unbelieving she flung open the door. Stepping through her head banging against the slanted bulk head.

Her knees hit the granite step, her body slumping against the jagged stone, laying limp from exhaustion. "I'm sorry. We tried," she whispered to her inner friend. Her eyes squinted at the beam of light exploding at her skull. Nathan knelt, bending to cover her. Moving her back to the bed, he caressed her. Some hours later and his head clear of pot and wine something in him was again responding. These feelings of remorse aren't normal. "What is happening?

Glendale Memorial was located on Center Street in Pembroke, closer to exit 2 off Route 3. After placing an elastic band at the base and securing a clean cloth with tape, the bleeding slowed considerably.

He considered traveling further away, perhaps Brockton or beyond, but that might cause someone to question his not seeking medical attention closer to home. Naturally he couldn't go to Monument.

His story. The surface edges of his work bench are covered with sheet metal. Attempting to move it on his own, he lost his grip. The sharp metal edge sliding down against his groin slicing him. The two shots of V O, and Tylenol, did nothing for the tooth-ache like throbbing of his dick. Pissing, a painful dilemma. Seeing his acute distress had outpatient nurses moving him instantly to a surgical unit. Pain medication administered by needle until Morphine injected into the I V.

The registration clerk, nurses and doctors outwardly accepted his explanation. His embarrassment reassuring them. He would remain overnight and the next day in order for doctors to evaluate, in addition to safeguarding against infection until healed sufficiently for reconstruction by a plastic surgeon. Nathan not pleased, but what was he to do?

He'd have to concoct a story for necessary time needed off work? He is due two weeks vacation, but had made plans to take a week at a time later on. He may have to explain the slower awkward walk, reducing tension in that area. A hernia! That's it. I have a hernia.

That would bring a question to some?  He could hear some smart ass nurse, "Why aren't you having Dr. Meyer do your hernia?"  Dr. Meyer being one of the finer surgeons at Monument.

"Oh, well, my cousin is a surgeon at Glendale. Keeping it in the family. You know?" That's what he'd say to smart ass.

Jan-Marie was curious after a week of going un-touched. He was unusually caring and kept his distance. That one time as he curled his arms around her from behind, she heard him winced uncomfortably. When she turned slightly, he pulled away and turned from her. "I have a small hernia, my sweet girl. Arousal seems to annoy it."

She comforted, hiding her grin, "Oh, sorry you are hurt."

He turned back. "I need day surgery in another week. Then I'll be fine after another three weeks or so?" He took her hand. "I can't wait. Please be a patient sexy thing."

In his semi-consciousness state he saw sweet Janine. She'll keep. He'd question Doc more closely tomorrow about healing time. Dreamy now, did he say something about a pill to keep it soft to heal?  He smiled. Reconstructing the tip gave him an added inch. Dreamy, his hand slipped around the   healing seven 7 inches. Marie will enjoy this!

# Chapter Nine

After dropping Jen, Dan returned coffee in hand to the apartment. He sat, pulled out an index and dialed up his F B I . Buddy, Joe La France. "Joe, Dan here. Yes it has been awhile. Good, and you sound well."

"Well the reason is I wonder if you could check for any info on unidentified recovery remains. Name, Janine Shepard, age twenty-eight. Attractive, blonde, five-seven, hundred twenty-two pounds give or take. No known scars, tattoos, markings. Your office or district should have received an original report a month or so ago when she first disappeared. Just calling to ask for a closer scrutiny of info. You know how it is. Okay my friend. Thanks, you to."

Dan sat, eyes scrolling the down the list of remaining female real estate agents listed in Mendelson and four towns bordering. Tedious, but if just one recalled being followed or noticed someone stopping, lurking, or something unusual over the past few months, it could have meant something. A stretch maybe, but would be more than zero, the nada they had now.

None of those he contacted this week was to provide anything. No flirting men,. . . or women. No weirdos showing up at their open houses. No particular vehicle seen repeatedly in the vicinity. A telephone voice of particular tone or quality wishing to speak several times with the same female Realtor. Dead ends. Nada! He headed for his car, list and street map of Carver in hand.

Dan bent over pretending to examine the passenger side tire. Looking each way without turning his hand slid into the partially opened mail box, fingertips pinching the edge of a lonely post card. This the reason the flag-up? It was a change of address form left for the rural carrier.

His memory not what it used to be, he quickly got in the car to scrawl the new Kingston address down. Mmm, interesting. If nothing else than simply moving for want of, at least it something to follow-on tomorrow.

Pulling down the road a bit from the box he flipped the atlas open to Kingston. Fingering down the index to Cedar Street referred you to area 9- J on the map indicated it off Manomet Avenue, a direction out of town near the Plymouth town line. In smaller print, Myles Standish Reservation. Speaking to the steering wheel. "Well Nathan Bass, let's clear you, then, and move on." The 'move-on' part in this statement stirred his mind to a more personal issue. Return home or stay and work on a relationship. He turned the car back toward Mendelson, and the diner.

Coffee and two scrambled put away, he kissed Jen as she stood at the register before a heading for his destination. Jen said to take route 44 to route 3 which would bring him to the south end section of Kingston.

Forty-minutes later fingering the larger scale map insert told him that Cedar Road turns onto a dirt road deep within a large acreage of forest in reservation land. He folded the map and sipping cold coffee headed slowly ahead. Dan hadn't passed one car yet on this section, every now and then a  narrow dirt road left or right where a cluster of several mail boxes stood, names scribbled or printed in assorted colors, most faded.

That last one read # 799, he thought. The faded 9, or 0?  He wanted 802. Idling along another road while questioning if  it a driveway, one box stood alone. Recently painted, #802.

Dan turned in, going carefully attempting to drive in the existing ruts, slowing to a stop to make it through areas washed out by rains. His luck will have him bottom-out, getting stuck, and eaten by ravaging coyotes. Or being confronted by an unknown cult-group at their dark forested hideaway. Far from lurking strangers.

"Come now," he muttered, at an estimated 200 feet in, and bushes getting heavier rubbing and squeaking against the car. Suddenly the tall pines not as closely cropped. The saplings and brush  spreading apart letting light in. The road became smoother from recently spread sand and gravel.

Just ahead a log cabin stood against a backdrop of darker forest. Dan pulled up next to a pick-up and hit the horn twice.

The axe swung high coming down to settle into the cutting stump. He saw a younger man in a blue hooded sweatshirt, jeans, Red Sox cap, heading over, led by a barking yellow Lab. "Hold up Lady. Take it easy. "

Turning in Dan's direction. "He won't bother you. Least if I'm here. What can I do for you?"

"Well my name is Dan. I'm with CSU Insurance. Canvassing homeowners in the area. My company offers fire, liability, homeowners, and hazard insurance type coverage. Most companies consider it more of a hazard for homes this far out being isolated from hydrants and distance from a fire station."

"Company assumes a larger risk. One might pay a bit higher premium, but not as much as with other companies. And most won't insure you at all. Anyway that's the reason for my driving in. Nice looking Lab."

"Yes she is. Rescued her from an abuser. You from around Mendelson? Although I suppose you were just eating at The Diner, when I saw you some time back."

This caught Dan off guard for the moment. "No, no, I'm from out of state. But cover three states in New England. Come this way when claims build-up, or sales from local agents decline, visiting to insure competitiveness. And yeah, I like to get out myself to sell if I can. Like meeting new bull shit sufficed.

"Well I'm all set with that stuff. I lived in Mendelson. Bought this place nearly two years ago. Was going to use it Summers, or for a get-away-week-end? Maybe rent it out a few weeks for some extra dough.

Then I decided to sell the place in Mendelson and make this my home. Nice, private, quiet. Moved in about seven months ago now. The Mendelson property is on the market."

"You picked an isolated spot for sure." Dan motioned his hand at the driveway. "Can see why you have the pick-up?"

"Yeah, I like it out here. The nicer neighbors are those you only occasionally wave to. He laughed.

Remembering now what that nice neighbor said. "Being out here, though must add to a commute to work?"

Nathan edged a bit on one foot. "Work just ten minutes away."

"Didn't look like a lot of business out this way?" Dan searching.

"There's a large Industrial Park between "Plymouth and Carver. I work at Monument."

Dan etched his head in question. A curious name. What sort of business is that?"

Nathan chuckled. "That's right, you the stranger. Monument Hospital."

In Dan's befriending nature, " maybe your right. Looking around "It is quiet. Well it was good talking with you," Dan hesitating for a response. "Oh, Nathan is my name." Good luck. Remember, take a left on Cedar."

Dan opened his door. "That farm in Mendelson? That all set with insurance? If vacant for long could be exposed to theft or fire from vagrants? That sort of thing?"

Nathan eager to be rid of this intruder on his day, kept walking raising his arm without turning. "All set! Have a nice day!" Returning in direction of the woodpile he glanced over his shoulder seeing

Dan's car now past the curve in the drive, darted to his truck with Lady trailing.

Pebbles flew as Nathan accelerated spinning rear tires. "Something about that guy? Better check the farm. The log-cabin his new home, he now referring to the Mendelson house as, the farm. "Sit Lady.

I didn't let you ride to climb all over the seats."

Dan felt a bit bummed-out with himself mumbling to his steering wheel, . . . "Am I losing my stuff? My god, man! Could have tried for more? Should have? Brought myself to a dead-end with that guy. Well, at least confirmed he moved from the farm, and where he works. He didn't appear edgy. Could have got more about what he does for work? Live alone? Who's the Realtor handling the farm?

He did walk a bit awkward coming from the wood stack! Was going to comment if he had pulled a muscle . . . or whatever? Then I forgot. I am getting rusty!

Although, his mind oddly wandering as it does, Jen says not, smiling at himself in the rear-view at the notion of a romantic interlude, . . . "come-on now, focus!" Theory of checking "loners" near complete. Unless another shows up, that's it.

Nathan followed three cars behind turning onto route 3 and soon onto route 44. "Looks like we're going to Mendelson, girl." Ladies' lids slid up but momentarily in reply.

Dan turned onto Plymouth and then Main. Nathan kept on Plymouth in direction of the farm.

A visual inspection outside found nothing unusual or changed since he had left. He went inside checking up and down. All secure, he returned to the truck and Kingston. Best not to be seen here. No sense in having nosey neighbors questioning. Or snoop-dog insurance men either.

"Hi Sweet Guy!" Dan smiled back at Jen behind the counter busy with the pie cutter. "You didn't call which. I assume, you found Kingston."

"Yes I did. But almost called you from within "the lost forest" deep in the dark outskirts of that town. By god it was like driving into an abyss. The sunlight disappeared. Huge oaks and pines suddenly took on awesome, eerie appearances bending over the dirt road making it even darker."

Humor in his tone, voice raised a pitch or two, eyes widening, "it was really, really scary."

Jen bent her head laughing, and too, embarrassed for him, customers turning, odd expressions distorting their faces.

He sat at the counter. She brought him coffee slipping her hand over his as her tongue licked her lips. She delivered a cup of minestrone her fingers tickling his palm eye winking. Two minutes later she served his the turkey club, touching her finger in the side of mayo before smoothing it on her lips, and smoothing it with the tip of her tongue.

In her best sultry voice whispered, "I'm off now. I'll walk home. Give you time to finish your lunch and me to shower and . . . you know; clean up and maybe throw on something . . . Comfortable. See you in half an hour big boy." She gave an extra kick to her hips as she swayed into the kitchen.

Dan stared, eyes embracing, holding her image though she was gone. Feeling arousal he spoke to the fork holding the first mouthful, "She makes me crazy!"

The following morning Dan sat sipping coffee, his mind adrift in thoughts of Jen. His lips held her taste, nostrils the smell of her skin and hair. He felt calm, at peace, and in love.

If she hadn't left for work, he would again bring her in as last night. Their lovemaking holding an intimacy. Nothing erotic, simple really. Wonderfully romantic. Sometimes tastefully to the edge of wild, yet respectful. Feelings intertwining in their very special bond.

# Chapter Ten

Joe Broderick stared out his office window focusing on Mrs. Barber doing one step at a time resting in between before carefully planting her cane on the next. Where and how would he be when in his eighties? She did this at least three times a week, two or three books under her left arm. Must read several a week?

Before he passed away nearly twenty years ago, Mr. Barber would be at her side. He had been head of maintenance for the school department for forty-five years. His masterful knowledge in electronics, furnace repair, and putting desks and chairs back together must have saved the town thousands of dollars.

Mark Barber had been a Special Officer with the police department for twenty years directing downtown traffic, the desk on a weekend now and again. And night patrols on Friday nights. Anyone in an auto accident late evening or early morning on a Friday met Mark Barber. He became proficient at first aid, assessing fault, and being wonderfully compassionate to those loved ones of a victim whom he met at the Out-patient department, the morgue, or after knocking at their door at two in the morning giving a family member grim news.

It's ironic that he would skid into a tree just past midnight one rainy night in October, and I knocking a half hour later to accompany his wife to the hospital, sitting with her at his bedside in Intensive Care. Mark re-gained consciousness but for a minute to smile his good-bye.

Joe suddenly thought of his wife Anne. Is their relationship aligned this way? He shook his head. Come on Joe, get to work! This is something he had to tell himself almost daily since the killing spree and kid-napping.

He popped a Paxil onto his tongue, sipped his orange juice. His being on an anxiety medication was between him and his longtime physician, Doctor Tranter. If Anne ever knew! It wouldn't have hurt to tell her he supposed. But he didn't wish her any worry. What bothered him was that they had no secrets.

And he wanted no one on the force or in town authority knowing.

Joe walked into the diner hoping to see Dan, and did. "Well, well. Still, in town huh? Ah, sweet love!"

"Hi Chief Joe! Stopping in for a complimentary breakfast? Isn't that what you local authorities call it?"

"There happens to be a strict rule agin it, "Joe retorted. "Anyway, not here to eat. Here to see you. Anything going on? Leads. Anything?"

"Well Joe, I'm sticking around because, well..."pointing at Jen's back. "In fact was going to check in with you later today. Everything's a dead-end."

"Okay. That's that then," the Chief rose off his chair dejected.

"Sorry Joe, "also dejected. "By the way I'll be leaving for a bit. But I'll be back. See you then."

"Thanks for the extra time spent, Dan. Have a safe trip."

Joe settled into the driver seat large fist slamming the steering wheel, "gaud-dam-it!" Feelings of incompetence filling him again. As his habit, he would chew on it awhile before concealing them deep within. Carry on, perform duties of Chief, thwart the pangs of guilt.

He and Anne shared everything. Consoling him in late or the wee hours after arriving home unable to sleep. The image of a teenager's semi-decapitated head through the windshield, half a car torn away by impact. Holding your stomach down prying loose the trigger finger of a distraught soul having splattered brain over the wallpaper.

The embarrassment as well. Several months now passing. Loved ones of victims had stopped calling

for updates. Maybe the nut case had moved on to murder elsewhere. Perhaps unknowingly, Dan or others investigating had scared him off.

Listen to Anne. Concentrate on today, like she says. If something breaks all well and good. He respected her advice. But how would those words be welcome by loved ones of the victims.

Those wishing for satisfaction perhaps. Not to speak of all those vulnerable to this monster. No doubt the  intermittent awakenings between one and three in the morning would continue.

He finished buckling his belt, sniffed and licked his fingers. Anyone watching reminded of a backyard dog.

"Remember the floor needs a sweep," he'd remind, and be gone. Maybe for a few days.

I collected plates and cups for the sink. Sheets soiled repeatedly over two days of his sweat and body fluids placed in with the rest of the wash. Afterward I scrubbed my hands under hot water with soap for five minutes.

Pacing until weary, I laid down . . .  Hoping the nightmares forgetting where I sleep.

She ran her hand over the fuzz on her head wondering how long before it would grow in again? To match the other side. He should have shaved it all, allowing it to grow back evenly. He made her wear a hat, hiding the top. The healing went well where he had stitched with fishing line. Thankfully done while she unconscious.

She could not keep food down from what she believed was a concussion?  She still had dizzy spells though not as frequent. And most thankfully, the nauseating head-aches subsided after two weeks.

She inwardly admitted he cared for her well, providing medicine for pain, cleaning the wound, and keeping her nourished, Soup mostly, for a time, due to the nausea. He even made her a special green tea with herbs.

His touch was gentler against her chin as he slipped spoonfuls of soup between her lips, holding the tea-cup to her mouth. He refrained from any sexual contact, not even mentioning it.

Until she was "ready", that is. Which he said she was a week ago. Gentle at first though in his wild way. Not so in the end.

She must endure . . . she must. She prayed for strength, her mind getting some from anger within. . .until the right opportunity . . .the right time.

"Lady-girl, do you still like her?  I mean,. . . .Are you tiring of her? Just a little?" He stopped at Curry's Variety for a box of dog treats and to pick up a new edition of Realty Magazine. It was time!  Or was it?

Dan, Jen and Angie settled in the car for their journey to Dan's home where they planned to spend five days. First priority on arrival to decide what to pack-up and load into the rented moving van . And secondly, sign a rental agreement with the couple before they're moving in. The unwanted items would be sold at a yard sale the day before driving back. With permission of the school Principal, Jen kept Angie out of school for the trip.

Nathan sat back against the shed, his jacket scraping old blistering paint to the ground. He spit out the chewed-up blade of grass from between his teeth staring now at the full page ad for Rustic Country Realty, OPEN HOUSES DONE RIGHT, catching his eye. Candace "Candy" Wright smiled back at him from lower left of the page. "Wow-ee Candy!"

Her appearance was striking. A blue suit playing harmony with a petite, tight and, oh so a sexy frame. Narrow face holding a sustained smile lit bright eyes sparkling within a halo of shoulder length blonde hair.

Eager to see if this little doll had a scheduled open house this weekend, he set out to buy a Gazette, stomach churning in anticipation. He was ready, and would have four days to scope and prep a plan. Suddenly somehow, out of nowhere, Jan's images stared back at him.

Life for Chief Broderick and his department returned to near normalcy. The routine of it anyway.

Days and nights turned back to investigating minor burglaries, domestic disputes, breaking up the occasional bar fight at Elmo's, and responding to traffic accidents and medical emergencies.

He rested back to swivel his chair before bringing the cup up. He had conquered the quirks of the chair, accustomed now to the spring action dipping right, jiggling the cup or powdered donut, sending him to the wash room, only to rub the stain larger. The spare uniform shirt hanging in the office closet, being one to air on the side of caution it remained on its hanger.

The killings evident in his thoughts daily, sneaking into a visit at different intervals. Like now, when alone. Attempting to conquer this he tried the "keeping busy" theory. Didn't work?

There was confrontation with himself, even when driving, the siren blaring, lights flashing, concentration on the road heightened. Eating breakfast within the midst of radio music and patron conversation.

He stood up at the thought, shook his head, grabbing his hat to head out for a drive. How could he have such thought? He cursed and swore slamming the rear exit door to the parking lot.

About to open his cruiser door, "Chief?" He turned. Gracie, today's dispatcher stood holding the door open. "Something the matter? Anything going on I should know?"

"Nothing Gracie. No concern. She smiled back. "Okay then." The door slammed by a stiff breeze.

He got behind the wheel. Good grief, confronted again by previous thought. How could he even ponder that another killing could in fact supply a clue! He withdrew the pill bottle from his jacket and started the engine.

"I told you to wait for me to help you!", Jen scolded seeing Dan positioned, one hand holding him up in a sitting position, the other feeling his lower back. It's just a spasm . . . I think. Give me a minute. Actually, come here, make fist," and pointing, "push in right here hard as you can." Jen complied. "Oh yeah, right there. Keep it right there. Yeah, oh yeah, right there!"

"Dan, stop your groaning like that! The neighbors we'll think we're making-out right here on the porch."

"That would be nice" he grimaced, a grasp on Jen to sit up. Resting his elbows on his knees momentarily he took in a breath before attempting a stretch, then slowly arched his back and forth slightly. "As I hoped, just a spasm. Think a couple of Ibuprofen in order though," as he walked stiffly through the front door, Jen placed a hand against his butt. "How about here? This need a rub too?"

"Funny, very funny. This subsides I'll guide your hand later." Jen gave her little "cooing" sound as she placed three Ibuprofen on the tip of her tongue. "This can be used as a dispenser." She sauntered up to him vivaciously swaying, slipping them between his lips.

Dan groaned, " It's cruel to tease a man when he's down."

"I know," she sympathized. Leaning in, " Doesn't feel like your down right here. That thing will never give up," she giggled. "Go rest awhile. Angie and I can carry on."

Dan opted for the rocker's hardness, self-doctoring it better for firmness rather than the possible displacement effects of soft sofa cushions. Within a few moments his head slumped, and he was in Mendelson. His mind traversing the murder scenes, interviewing contacts, and photo images. He scanned the reports, the lists of locals having any probable connections. Even in the serenity of a dream, no clues surfaced. No sudden "hit yeah right in the eye" fresh lead, as can happen.

Awake he stretched, thankful that aside from minor stiffness, the pain had reduced to a twinge. He now concluded it was indeed a pulled muscle. "Hey you two, I'm back in action".

# Chapter Eleven

"Hello. Joe Montane Mr. Wilkes. Received the package on Mrs. Bass. I have a flight booked for Florida. Just wanted to convey I've started. Will do, and thank you for the business."

Joe had worked for three insurance companies since graduating from college ,and now celebrating his forty-eighth birthday. That was five years ago. He had worked in-house with Montauck in New Jersey, and as field investigator with Washington General and Federal Funded. He gained recognition through the years for saving his companies hundreds of thousands in claims. Either in proving suicide versus natural death, out-right fraud, or accidental deaths not being quite so, accidental.

The morning after turning forty-eight is when he sat with Pamela, wife of twenty years, and came to a decision to venture out on his own, forming Montane Associates. Pam ran the office, which was less than part-time really. Joe never took on more than two cases at a time and remained the lone investigator. He contemplated having another, but couldn't convince himself that anyone could do as adequate a job as himself.

This current case required travel to Florida being hired by Massachusetts Alliance to look into the death of one Marie Patterson Bass. Alliance issued a life policy three years earlier for $750,000.00. Ms. Bass allegedly died in a drowning accident in Marina Bay, off the shores of St Augustine.

He scanned the file again on the plane. No suspicious findings by police, etc. Manager of Claims at Mass Alliance ordering a report due to the policy amount. And too, wanting to verify witness accounts of the "tripping" incident causing her falling overboard. Only witnesses to this "trip", a guy in his late twenties who happened to be walking his dog just one boat ramp over.

He stared at a police photo of the body. Her head visible above the white sheet laying on a wooden dock. "Well Marie, I'll concentrate on the one witness, and search the marina for more. Want to re-check with authorities on their officer's and autopsy report.

The primary beneficiary was changed two years ago after husband James Bass made her a widow. That was when living in Mass. She then assigned a sibling, Samantha Paine living in Tempe, Arizona.

A handsome sum of dough, he thought. But it is term insurance, and at her age then forty-three could still purchase at a reasonable rate on a preferred basis. Assuming she did it to protect her estate and family from debts, and whatever other expenses. She had good business sense to purchase at affordable premiums.

So how would I contact this witness? The police report had a name, Benny Goodwin. He told police what he observed that early evening, and that was that, as far as the report went. This guy gave a temporary address of the Palms Motel on Crescent Avenue. Said he vacationing, visiting old college friends. No permanent address on the police report? Did they bother to ask? Wonder if the Palms requests good info from their guests?

The autopsy report concluded cause of death as drowning. Accidental drowning. Contributing factors. Head trauma, a gash at a frontal lobe area, a second at the rear neck line. Blood was found on the brass rail running the side deck. Nothing to conclusively distinguish which resulted from contact with the rail or some object underwater.

Hopeful he would gather sufficient findings or, as in some instances, not enough, to conclude this matter for Alliance. He rested his back against the soft pillow placed by the attendant, eyes wanting to nap. But not before glancing down at the last page of the report. Mendelson. Joe's gaze shifted out the plane's oval window. Not having checked he wondered now if it located near Boston, or maybe the Cape? Albeit something he wished not requiring that find out.

The pink Bic touched the end of the Salem Candace held between her lips. Her hand brushed the first smokey cloud away while her backside fell comfortably against her office window ledge. Spotting an elderly woman vacating the park bench next to her office, she swiftly took a seat. She would have sat with that woman, for she didn't mind chatting, but from past experience did not wish "making friendly" with someone's pooch trying to bite her shoe, or worse, sniffing between her legs.

She remembered back when working alone in her office, smoking inside, having a scotch at her desk after a long day. She still would, if not for hiring Mary Lou, her part-time office clerk, and Sheri Goodstone, a Realtor working a three-day week, some selling, but mostly handling bank closings and the paper work with prospective buyers. She enjoyed that end of the business and for performing it ambitiously, forgoing commission work, I supplemented her pay.

Candace preferred being out, prospecting, setting up sales, meeting new people and showing open houses. Sheri would be house-sitter occasionally if Candace had week-end plans. Since her divorce though, Candace spent most week-ends alone. Her marriage had not resulted in motherhood. She really never wanted children. Her ex, Matt after three years married did. Things became irritable at home, something she didn't need in her personal quest to have the top Realty office in the area.

Thus, the divorce three years in. Matt wasted little time meeting someone two towns over and lives happily with Mona and three sons. Candace even admitting, Mona a really nice woman and mother. And, yes, wife. She still remembered the awkward situation selling them the home they now occupy.

She pressed what remained of the Salem in what had become her portable ash tray held in her hand while rising to open the office door.

"Look at her Lady. That red skirt brings out her dark hair and green eyes. And those legs long and lean leading to . . . wow! Not bad for what, thirty-five-ish, maybe thirty-eight." Still looking for a last glimpse through the large window, he started the truck.

Nathan's plans had come to fruition. The extra room made-over for Jan-Marie, as he preferred calling her, having been completed. He had spared no expense. The walls were 8" thick, insulation 6", studded walls held ½" plywood covered with oak panels. A large room combined bedroom and bath. An oversized bath with shower, sink, and toilet. Bed, two night stands, dresser. A Victorian styled desk set all matching Mahogany. A HDTV hung on the wall. The smaller room held a washer/dryer, small refrigerator, microwave, sink, and two cabinets. Quite sufficient when she alone. Meal-times were most often spent together.

He felt more at ease here isolated in these dark woods. Over many months he had also come to endear this woman he had originally planned to kill. More so after she had nearly killed him.  In some strange way he came to feel attached somehow. She was certainly lovely. Imagine, lovely! He would smile. Not fucking material?  A nice ass! Legs!

If her hair was brown, skin lighter, a bit shorter in height, she was Mamma in that picture on the shelf.  When he approached her in the evenings as she lay curled, she did not fight. Her hands came around him as he slid against her. She says nothing, but that is okay. They speak at meals or when she in his company in the main house.

A major condition remained. Ridding the past. Not the family history. For that he cherished. The more recent history held within that cellar had moved with him, and apart of the present. The insurance money certainly a welcomed aspect.

He was not seen around there in some time. It had been for sale. Though he gave no  encouragement when Realtors or interested parties stopped by. He would offer excuses, a change of heart about selling, etc.

He grew very accustomed to having Jan-Marie around. He sometimes fought inside what she really meant to him. Has he fallen in love?  She had certainly affected his postponing Open-House plans. Although inside that urgency lurked, teasing, pulling. The excitement. The revenge so sweet. Why not so with her . . . look at her so peaceful. Hating to wake her. . . . His robe fell to the floor.

Her eyes opened to his blurry image. As became his ritual, he would lay beside me gently stroking my hair before moving to follow my spinal line three fingers slowly moving over each bony disc from neck to the crevice at my behind. And then the same fingers on their upward path. After three or four minutes his breathing would increase a bit, his leg would fall against mine, those fingers following the crevice, one finger now probing between my thighs.

His body would then bend. His lips kissing my behind, my thighs. "Roll over my sweet," he would whisper. And like a robot I had become,

I would respond. He would do whatever pleased him. I, though, provided no emotion, nor gained anything from these moments. Periods of blurred vision overshadowing reality.

Nathan was aware of the reason for her calming affection. Janine's awareness of being alive. Her mind and being accepting terms. His terms. Why?

# Chapter Twelve

When the first apparatus arrived, full concentration focused on the house as was procedure. The barn stood ten feet away. Firefighters proceeded inside once part of the nearly destroyed structure allowed. Their search found no bodies. The barn, no carcass. Neighbors interviewed at the scene, thought it vacant for some time.

The State Fire Marshall arrived at seven a.m. Preliminary findings that it started in the barn near the wall closest to the house. Beer bottles, a condom package inside one, and evidence of smoking outside pointed to a teen party. No evidence of gasoline storage, or other chemicals were found.

Ownership records would be verified in the morning. The Fire Chief spoke met up with Chief Broderick on the scene. "Mike, you can double check, but last known the son, Nathan Bass the listed owner. And that several months ago, nearly a year now, maybe. I didn't notice the ' For Sale' sign tonight. But am pretty sure this property was on the market. Kid moved to Kingston last known. Dan, you remember, the guy you met with me at the sation one day. He tracked this Nathan to Kingston during his investigation of the Realtor murders."

"You have his number, Joe? I'll call him for Bass's address. Your guys are calling on the neighbors. I'm sure the Fire Marshall would like to speak with this guy as part of the investigation. Right now, appear teenagers having themselves a good time. Well talk to you later Joe."

"Thanks Mike. And thank your guys. And oh, Helen your new on-call. She worked like a . . . .Better watch what I say, or how said. I'll have a night guy swing by here later. Make sure it didn't re-flame."

Mike was tossing his boots into his town pick-up, "thanks for that, Joe. I'll be with Ed in the morning to complete a walk and sift through. Join in, if you have time."

Joe gave a wave of his arm.

Well Lady, you were perfect. Performed just as trained. You balanced that all that way and then inside to the wall where your treat waited for you in the dried hay. Imagine! A dog arsonist.

No footprints, no tire treads, no chemicals, anywhere near the place. And fortunately, no passers-by as we walked the fields to the truck.

He laughed aloud, "just those crazy kids having a party in the barn. Of course my finding teen party evidence from the night before was luck, and my good Lady dropping that condom-in-a -bottle for the finding."

Self-satisfied Nathan sucked a gulp of beer before pouring Lady's share into her dish. Also, as planned, he and Lady sat parked for nearly an hour waiting patiently for the lights upstairs at the Fire station to come on and the large doors slowly rise to the sound of the horn and the roar of the first engine.

Nothing was found at the site post-fire investigation. Nor did neighbors have anything to contribute. Several pointing out, to Nathan's good fortune, that kids were always partying on the property.

"Told the cops more than twice. Not surprised!" Their common remark.

Even though nothing suspicious found to confirm arson, the property owner Nathan Bass, was contacted and interviewed at the Mendelson station. His demeanor conveyed that he visibly upset at the loss. Otherwise, he was the picture of calm when questioned. He was at his new home in Plymouth. There no reason to question otherwise.

The property was insured for $225,000.00, that including the barn, house, two sheds, farm equipment, and personal property. It was originally insured for $450,000.00. The ENIAC Insurance Company downgrading the amount, due to decline of care and other risk factors. If knowing the property vacant probably would have cancelled the policy.

In fact, seeing this recorded in the Fire Marshall's report, and as uncovered by their own investigator, could deny the claim. Although this unlikely. Subsequent files by Mr. Bass's attorney stating that his client, although moving to a new address, had someone caring for the property.

A Mr. Simpson did hay of one field and so on. Of course Mr. Simpson wanted no part of having to contribute statements. And actually hadn't lived there.

In the end Nathan and his attorney opted for the settlement offer by ENIAC, of $150,000.00. Nathan accepting his share of $135,000.00, smiling all the way to his recently established savings account at The Pilgrim Savings and Loan.

Chief Broderick sat opposite Barbara Jenks in the end booth at the Diner. He had offered her dinner at The Wells, an upscale restaurant out on Route 28, to which she declined. She had eaten at the Diner once before with Joe, and decided again this the atmosphere that suited her, as well as their topic of conversation.

She and Joe had spoken often by phone and by e-mail about her sister, Janine Shepard. Nearly a year passing, had Barbara calling the Chief for another meeting. Some advice, she said on the phone. This startled Joe, for she was not well taken with the very limited information and evidence since her sister's disappearance.

"Barbara, again, if you want to hire someone, well and good. I told you this before. As I also told you, the FBI, our department, along with others surrounding us. And, yes, I called in a private investigator, who is also a friend."

Barbara eyed him with surprise on her face. "Chief you never told me that!"

"I know. No one knew but me at first. Later, a few area Chiefs and two of my men were informed. Sometimes when cases go cold, as we say, it is advantageous to call in an unknown to work locally. No notoriety and things settling down, at least outwardly, sometimes gives the culprits a sense of accomplishment. They let their guard down.

"As we've discussed before, this kidnaping appears to be by a person or persons with no financial goals in mind. Janine had no enemies. She was an attractive, vibrant woman. I have been quite truthful in telling you before that most cases such as this, whether planned or unplanned, do not end well for the family. A sexual predator, a nut-case with some personal avenges to feed his warped mind. And again,"

Barbara stopped his words with her palm lifting. Joe, you and your people, . . . well I've said it all before. The reason I came was to ask your advice whether to hire someone. Someone fresh, from out of the area, to start from the beginning. Investigate where no one has with a fresh mind, fresh eyes. A moment ago you let on that you had an outside investigator. I wish I had known. I assume, then, this fellow failed to uncover anything new?"

"That is so. And he is from out of the area. A retired FBI guy. Real good too. But, he isn't exactly finished. He still comes out this way a couple times a month. Pokes around some more. The other reason for his 'timely visits', which may be turning into 'more often visits', is that during the past year he began seeing Jen, our waitress. It has blossomed into a special relationship."

Joe sipped his coffee. "Anyway, I suppose I should have trusted you with that information, and saving you this. Although I never mind seeing you. Talking about the case. And your special relationship with Janine."

Barbara smiled into his eyes. "Thank you again Chief Joe Broderick. I better get started." Joe slid out standing and extending his hand. "I'll be talking with that fellow. Dan is his name. Tell him about you, Barbara."

She dismissed his hand to fold her arms around him,, and whisper into his chest. "Your words, your eyes, tell me this has not been easy. You have those other victims' families on your mind as well." She stood away, lifting her smile, "Don't let it destroy you. Joe. Call me when you can." Joe nodded, his eyes telling her that he would. He sat back down. There is a woman who has every right to be outraged. At me, at law enforcement, at the world in general. And surely she has been. The strength some exhibit. The beat of despair drummed in his stomach. He emptied his cup, grabbed his hat, "come on now, listen to yourself. Listen to the words of encouragement from her, from everyone."

Dan poured the fresh brewed into his cup, picked up his cell pressing speed dial.

"Hello, you. Do you realize the time? And what day this is?"

"Oh hell! I'm sorry sweetie. It's Wednesday. You have the day off. And I thought you'd be stepping out of the shower about now talking dripping wet. Mmm . . . mmm!"

"You are a jerk sometimes. But I love it. So what's so important?"

"Signed an agreement on the house later last night. Had a couple drinks and pizza with Jack. I think he was just a little upset having agreed to reduce the price, and therefore his commission by one-percent. Then to have two couples loving the house, and the Jamison couple upping their offer. So I made an extra $3,000, and with his one-percent off, another $2500. Some times life is fair. Was late when I got home, so waited to call you until now? What do you think?"

"That's wonderful Dan. So where do you plan on moving to?"

"Well, let me see. It was not long ago when speaking to a young lady from Massachusetts, a beautiful and quite sexy gal as I recall, that some pretty formative plan laid out. If that plan has somehow been forgotten, or changed, then. . . ."

"Listen, you, get your ass in your car and drive here right now. Better yet. Fly out. We can get your car and what remains there after you pass papers. Let's hope these kids have the dough."

"According to their Realtor who was finding them a property, they were pre-approved. And you know, I'm hanging up to call the airline right now. Love you!"

Jen pulled the sheets up, speaking to them, "I suppose this place is big enough."

# Chapter Thirteen

Nathan's eyes hadn't left her sleekness from the time Candace first positioned herself in the white rocker on the front porch, crossing a long and tanned bare leg over the other. His mind speaking, "She is a beauty." His thoughts feeding imagination, feeling her thigh, his hand slowly stroking back and forth, eager to explore. His mouth sucked at her neck, lips quivering impatiently with desire to search lower.

The rocker hitting against the siding, brought him back. Her hands moved slowly down each hip and thigh smoothing any wrinkle. Nathan suddenly realized that his mind desired her . . . wanted . . . Could actually feel and smell her tanned moothness. Yet his body was not physically reacting. His hand reached . . . only a partial? Only seconds out of his imaging he had only partial eagerness to go after her?

His fingers turned the ignition. Another day my sweet. Janine-Marie stared from the back seat. He turned seeing only smooth polished leather.

Joe Montane enjoyed travel, larger cities, nice hotels, and good food. If he was going to have to earn a living this way why not, at least most of the time. It had not always been this way. Eating fast foods and putting in for three times that, for extra pocket money. Driving a small rental, staying in dives and conniving the desk clerk at a Marriot for a fake receipt. No more, no way. Especially since having a better built a better reputation than most.

He had flown to T F Green Airport in Providence. His realizing, after making the reservation that this his first time here. The black Lexus rental sailed smoothly along Route 95 heading to connect with Route 495 South and closer to Mendelson. His Blackberry informed him the closest thing to a Marriot within fifteen minutes of Mendelson would be a Days Inn. Oh, the reality of it. Re-visiting the screen, well, the Tuscan House Ad menu, dining room and lounge photos look inviting, and just minutes from the hotel.

He then laughed aloud, " listen to me? The spoiled one, enabling himself."

The heavy door opened, the bottom sounding the familiar screech over the cement floor.  As she so often thought before, she hoped it late, and that he too tired to visit . .

…..To desire her.

The light coming on blinded her for an instant. "My sweet thing, you are awake. I've put the kettle on. Come join me upstairs for tea and peanut butter cookies. Or do you prefer milk, as often you do?"  Jan aroused sitting up in the bed. "Tea is fine, James."

She had learned well to call him James, not Jim. He would prefer Nathan, but . . . always cover thyself.  He took her hand, as she had grown accustomed, leading her up the stairs and into the kitchen.  She often, at these times, felt the urge to resist. As instantly such thought produced, it vanished, as if never there. So strange. About to think on something, and then feeling as if it never there.

As always the small dessert place settings and cloth napkins arranged just so. Fine china tea cups, perhaps antique, sitting on small circular doilies in their saucers. And those two tall white candles flickering tiny shadows on the white linen table covering.

After seating her he sat studying her for the moment, until her head prompted a look. He turned away attention to lifting the steaming tea, strings from three bags having steeped perfectly. "My mother preferred tea brewed in a ceramic pot. I'm sorry, Jan-Marie. Sorry for repeating myself."

She declined an answer, simply doling a smile. She thought James exhibiting peculiar looks toward her. Sipping tea, biting his cookie without the fanfare often displayed, seemingly out of pure excitement of the moment. Bordering on joyous really. Tonight though he is unfocused. Here, then not. Something heavy in mind perhaps. This better than my lonesome doldrums setting.

"Here dear, don't forget this special cookie. The one you must eat, as always.  Tomorrow I'm baking those special brownies you like," muttering,  . . . Must enjoy. They are so good for you."

Jen and Angie were late for Dan's flight due to land at 5:29. Luckily getting a space on the first level of the garage, they sprinted to arrival gate, and the baggage claim area. Angie shouted from several steps ahead, "there you are. Hi Dan!" Jen slowed down. He was in conversation with a blonde ten years, at least, his junior. Platinum hair shoulder length, tight fitting blue skirt six inches above the knee. Make-up impeccable and smile to die for.

Angie hugged him. Dan's head turned searching. He quickly motioned with his arms toward me. Then came running to me, like a military man home after 2 years away. His strong arms enfolded me, lifting me. "O how I've missed you, and thought of this moment every mile on that plane."

I smiled near usual. "Jen, sweetie, what is it" My glance over his shoulder answered. He grabbed my arm walking me to this babe and Angie. Before he could speak, Angie intervened. "Mom, this is Dan's sister, Madeline. She joined him on his flight. She has business in Boston. Wow, huh!"

Jen felt her face warming. Madeline's hand came forward. "After that flight I feel I know you already." Jen squeezed back. "Dan never mentioned his sister traveling with him. And how attractive she is."

"You are quite kind, Jen. And this maneuver was last minute. We actually bumped into one another in Pittsburgh where we each had a lay-over for an hour. Talk about coincidences. Our connecting flight was the same. Dan has told me, how shall I say, close you have become. I think it's wonderful.

I told Dan earlier that I would like to take you all to dinner, my treat. I've been this way before, and know The Capitol Grille in Providence. A fine meal to be had by all. I can pick up my rental later." Her smile seemed captivating.

I looked down at my jeans and older boots. "Never you mind ten. I've got a spare jacket in my bag. They'll accept us or else." Dan gave Jen a look. "The head waiter won't dare the Madeline-wrath upon himself, believe me." All laughing, they headed for the garage.

After a wonderful, and lengthy dinner, they dropped Madeline back at the airport car rental. Saw her off on her way to Boston, she accepting the invitation to stay with them in Mendelson, if her business complete.

"So what do you think of her? My fake sister, that is. Pretty sexy huh?"

A quick elbow to his rib section, " I knew all along, the moment I saw her," Jen boasted. "Yeah, right. I saw the questioning in those pretty eyes of yours, Jennifer."

"She certainly is attractive. Smart and dependent, huh," Dan.

"That she is. Been that way since high school. Her junior year. Before that was pretty much quiet, withdrawn even. Her history teacher, Mrs. Flemington had an influence on her. Maddie, as she then called. They really took to each other. Of course all the guys referred to her as The Flem. Sounds corny now."

"Anyway, Maddie joined the Drama Club at the urging of Flem, who also headed the club. Maddie took to it after awhile, overcoming, or at least dealing with shyness. And who knew she had a good singing voice. She had lead role as Maria in the Sound Of Music Junior year, and in the Spring of her Senior year, her second Maria role in West Side Story. My mom and dad were so proud. From their she went on to college filling herself with dependence, flair, and intelligence."

Her own Marketing Company, I can't imagine, Jen contended.

Dan cricked his head, "it all didn't just happen. She drove herself, especially after Rick died in that accident she spoke of. Was motivated before, but after . . . well?"

Angie awoke as they pulled into the driveway. She was washed and in bed within ten minutes. After showering together Dan carried Jen crossing the hard tile onto the soft texture of the bedroom carpet. They held each other under satin sheets.

Joe Montane, never one to waste time, signed in at the hotel and walked into The House Restaurant ten minutes later. His pallet prompted a nice juicy sirloin of beef, accompanied by a nice Pinot Noir. First though a solid hit of Dewars on the rocks, maybe two.

He told Katie, the attractive blonde, and way-too-young-for-him hostess, that he preferred one of the booths on the side of the room where a row of oversized windows ran the length. Instructions to give him about thirty minutes to unwind in the lounge. She placed his name for booth four, thirty minutes.

Mike, the bartender slapped a napkin down, poured the Dewars, and asked if he needed a menu. "Got a booth in dining half an hour.

Thanks though." Mike observed Joe's sideway glance follow the movement of the brunette waitress.

"Maybe you should have opted to eat at a table in here. Kiara, her name. A real nice person. And, yeah that too. The hostess and she are sisters. Katie may be available. But if anyone has the wrong thing in mind will deal with me. Kiara is taken. In fact Jason often stops in on his way home. Sneak a few moments with her, and down a beer or two. I'll run your tab to your waitress. Enjoy your dinner."

Joe sat on the side of the booth facing the entrance to the dining room. He always did. The menu spread open, his mind dueling between the Sirloin and the Filet. He always did. Then too, as most often did, would opt for his favorite, Sirloin.

A nice meal, fine wine, and back to his room. Work begins tomorrow here in Mendelson, Mass.

The Diner was extra busy this morning. Sixteen-year-old Willie standing at the ready clearing and cleaning as soon as a patron left a table. Jen and her partner waitress busy running back and forth.

Dan and Angie had decided earlier to breakfast out this morning. Spotting a couple at the far end of the counter readying to pay their tab, he checked the others waiting. They appeared in groups of more than two. To be safe, and courteous, he asked aloud if anyone waiting for two. Two heads went side to side, one guy said four.

An older fellow was alone, but motioned forward. "Go on you two. I see Pete there about ready." Pete heard, his head motioning up and down while draining the good to the last drop from his mug.

Jen rushed by dropping a moist wipe, a blank slip and pencil onto the counter, "give the counter a wipe and write your order."

Dan smiled at Angie, "I'll wipe, you write. Ham and two eggs medium for me, and whatever you're having. Think she'll remember coffee and a chocolate milk on her own?" They laughed aloud, then louder seeing the smirk on the face of their waitress.

"My feet are already killing me and I've got three more hours of this. Which means you two, that the apartment should be vacuumed, dusted, and at least two wash cycles done and dried by the time I arrive home. Enjoy your meals." She made a huff-sound, and shuffled away without one turn-back.

Trying to contain laughing louder, napkins suddenly covered their mouths, preventing home-fries spurting onto the counter. Dan choked out a whisper,"we're going to be in for it later." This remark making the moment worse. Now people around them were laughing. One red-faced waitress's face loomed large in the opening from the kitchen. All laughing stopped. Then it was Jen's turn. Her smile disappearing as she turned to a pick-up order.

Angie looked seriously at this man she liked. "You love my Mother, Dan?

Dan set his fork onto his plate. Eyes focused into Angie's, "So very much. So very much. And I have come to love you as well." His arm came around her as she leaned into his side.   A red-faced waitress, eavesdropping and writing an order, stopped. She felt her heart move. Feeling overjoyed, she had the urge to shout . . . . . .

Dan vacuumed, Angie dusted and mopped. He threw clothes from the washing machine into the dryer, she re-filled the washing machine. Angie left to walk to meet a friend at the Library.   Dan seated himself in the comfort of the leather chair. A stack of local Gazettes sat saved on the ottoman.

Setting the glass of ice tea on the table, he slid his readers on, and started from the oldest of two weeks ago. Three down, he unfolded showing the front page. The large lettering part of the headline, "FIRE," catching his attention.  Reading the article, 'The old Bass farm. . .  Plymouth Street . . .  barn, house, only sheds left standing. . . .Fire Marshall's findings' negative for arson . . . partying teens suspected . . . .

Dan re-read every word, images reeling in picturing the days he was there. "Wow, he said aloud.  "That a wow for me?" Jen sauntered in taking the place of the paper in his lap.   "From the look on your face, the wow not for me."

"You always wow me, you know that. No, I was catching up on the Mendelson news. Came across the article about the fire. You never mentioned it in our phone calls while I was back home."

"Guess I didn't think of it. Any special reasons I should have?"

"Well I suppose not. Remember back just over a year now I think, I asked you about this young guy Bass. Nathan Bass. Kind of a loner you thought, at the time. Well later on I confided in you the reasons for my interest. I guess right now my investigatory mind is kicking in. My suspicious mind, that is."

Jen pulled her knees up, inched her head nuzzling Dan's neck but for a moment before covering his mouth with hers, accompanied by a sensuous moan. Any thought of the article, or anything else, lost.

Chief Joe Broderick shook Joe Montane's hand before motioning an invitation to the chair next to his desk, and poured into two coffee mugs.

"They're clean, Mr. Montane. Washed daily. Got six of them. Normally mine the only one used. I keep them on hand for visitors like you. I prefer them to Styrofoam."

"Just like a drink. Wine especially, is meant to be served in a sparkling clean wine glass, Champagne in a glass flute. Scotch on the rocks, Martini, you name it . . . In a glass. I know it's extra doing at a cook-out, for example, but it's meant to be."

Deciding he'd better, visitor Joe took a sip.

The Chief took his seat. "Well I digress, Joe. Info on the former Mrs. Bass you said. The second one that is. Marie, right?"

"That's right Chief Broderick," being polite. Pausing a second, expecting a "call me Joe" back at him, but didn't. He continued. "Chief, Marie Bass's life was insured with Alliance, the company who hired me. You know, to keep things tidy, no loose ends before pay-out. Especially an accidental death situation. Double Indemnity. Did you know this woman? If not, you might refer me to any who did.

The closer the better."

"I knew Marie as a local Realtor in town. In her company a few times, attending a function or Rotarian Club lunch? That sort of thing. Never heard anything negative, certainly nothing criminal, to set that record straight. She was personable, somewhat attractive in that she kept herself a neat, dressed well."

Joe stretched before lifting his cup and setting it down. "There was the usual gossip about town how she could be somewhat demanding in her business life. But, hey, that's business. Then the other thing when she and Jimbo Bass started seeing one another. Although like anything that faded quickly."

"Some people's opinion she took him for a little ride. I knew James, Jimbo as he was called. A real nice man. Hard working, quiet. The two together didn't, on the outside at least, fit. Hey, who to judge, I say. Well, try not to in most cases."

Chief Joe picked up on the visitor Joe fidgeting a bit. "Oh yeah, someone who might . . . there is the son, Nathan, of course. As I understand it, or as rumored, he lived away for some time. Returned when his mother passed. A sweeter woman one could meet. He went away for a while. Returned when Jimbo died. Kid was very broken-up losing his father. And even more so when the mother went. Word was he not fond of the second Mrs. Bass. Seems a larger section of the farm acreage sold to the town under the Wetlands Act. That only left a few acres and the house to Nathan."

The Chief hesitated, "This might save you some time. My investigator, Dan Hudson checked out the son to a degree. Thinks he smelled something. Has a notion. But really can't pin anything down. Checked with Monument Hospital administration. Clean employment records.

Montane sat up leaning on the edge of the chair. The word motive chimed in his head. "Really. And why Chief? Do you think?"

"A larger section of the farm acreage was sold in a deal with the Town under the Wetland Conservation Act, leaving a few acres and the house, which Nathan inherited when Jimbo died. Maria        Moved relocated to Florida. Word of her death did reach back here. Some boating accident?"

"Right Chief. But was it an accident? Alliance wants to iron it out, so to speak.

"Thanks Chief Broderick, for your time. I'll be nosing around here for a few days, should anyone call about some nut asking questions."

"Take care Montane, I mean", . . .

Montane turned, "Chief, I'm used to it. Lots of folks latch onto the Montane thing. Maybe it suits my demeanor, or profession. You know, 'Montane, P. I'. The movie character, 'Bond,' or T.V.'s 'Magnum'. Oh well, and with a wave, the door to the station buzzed-open.

That woman . . . at her desk . . . is that me? . . . Working the computer? The large glass window lettering, . . . REAL ESTATE. Only her dreams held this familiarity. Reality fading. Nearly gone . . . Nearly. The door! "I'm back sweet darling Jan-Marie!"

# Chapter Fourteen

After walking the ruins and ashes of what remained of the barn and house, Dan's backside rested against the bark of the shade tree. The same from over a year ago, his mind imaging as it always did. He sniffed a soft breeze. The powdery scent, then replaced by the dank smell of charcoal.

That fragrance, he had smelled it this morning. On the way from the back patio to the car. The heat from the dryer vent spewed the same.

He walked over the ashes again trying to remember the set-up. Was there a bulkhead? A basement? The inside, as recalled had no washer / dryer room. If only he could be definite. It must have come from the cellar. Back then one couldn't tell. Now though the floors had collapsed into the basement, outlined by a foundation.

Why would a seemingly vacant house have the smell of a fabric softener sheet filling the yard? Dan's mind began rapid firing. He jumped five feet or so lading on rubble surrounded by old stone. Eyes focused at what his shoes kicked at.

In the corner sticking partially between burnt flooring and stone, something peeling white. He walked, dodging nails face-up in old lumber. There the remnants of a dryer, and spun-wire from a dryer hose.

"Chief? Dan. I'm at the burnt out Bass place on Plymouth Street. Got something to show you. I'll be here." Dan angled some of the longer 2x6's only charred a bit, against the stone foundation. Maintaining balance, he slowly stepped out of the rubble.

He had slumped under that tree but five minutes when Joe's siren signaled arrival.

"I didn't say I found a body!", Dan laughed at the Chief.

"Didn't want to have you been waiting on me? Beside you sounded a bit startled. Especially for a Pro."

Dan's hand grabbed his crotch. Grinning. "Pro this."

Joe was quick, "small, amateur stuff, you mean"

"So what is it? Well Joe, remember my paying this place a visit? In fact I called from here asking if you knew the place. Which you did. Your suggestions sent me to the Assessor's office. Remember?"

"I do in fact. But what about now?"


"Well, when here, I got whiffs of a fragrant or powdery smell. Dismissed it then. Today, I recalled that, and compared it to the same smell coming from the dryer vent at the apartment. You know those fabric softener sheets Anne tosses into the dryer. Climbing back down he boards. "Look, Joe," holding up the dryer vent wire, and pointing to the top of a dryer.

"Looks like the house may have been vacant, but the basement may have been used."

"Dan, you may be reacting too, . . . I know, you're the pro here! Well, I mean, hey the kid, Nathan. Maybe he was living in the basement cause the place was a mess? Or he came here to wash and dry his clothes. Say, while the house in Kingston built."

Dan's exuberant expression fell to bleak. "Talk about knocking a guy down Joe. You're a master. A fucking master!" Dan kicked at a pile of rubble which lifted into a breeze. This small cloud of soft white and gray ash caught them both. Each turned spitting, moving in opposite directions, arms waving, hands slapping at ash on their clothes.

" Dumb-ass Dan! What were you thinking?"

"Thanks for the ass remark, my good friend. And obviously, I wasn't thinking. I was reacting in temper! I sometimes do. And I enjoy doing it, even if it wrong."

Joe fell against the old foundation bent over choking on laughter. As he stood straight a shoe hit him square in the chest. "How's that Chief?" Dan landed on his ass. Laughing like a school-by, unable to get himself up.

Joe looked around, thankful. "Imagine anyone witnessing this scene!" This statement simply adding to the foolishness of good friends.

A moment later each headed in the direction of home and a welcomed shower.

He cradled Lady before him. Hand over her mouth. "What are they doing, girl?," slight nervous edge to his words? Tall grass and low branches hid them well. But why their laughter? Maybe Candace will draw them away . . . By clue perhaps left haphazardly behind. Albeit, unnatural for this "phantom." He smiled to himself. This cunningness coming forth, in hiding these past months excited yet withdrew him away . . . again imaged Jan-Marie. "Come Lady . . . Sssh, stay low. We must plan, even if it feel not quite" . . . . .

Joe Montane was at wit's end. Three days having passed speaking to the Chief, the Assessors office, Towns clerk who married Jimbo and Marie. Those three neighbors on Plymouth. The Fire Chief.

He mumbled a lot when alone. "To Kingston then, the kid. Kid ? He must be thirty-five! Suddenly incite kicked his sub-conscious in play. . . . Thirty-five, and owns a DOG!"

"Yeah I know it sounds like a dumb question, Carl. But, I'd like to find out, if possible. The officers questioned the guy might recall. They questioned him at the pier. Get a description of the guy. He was walking a dog. Get hold of the officer and ask him. Was it a yellow Lab? What could it hurt? Thanks Carl."

Montane sat back, snapping the cap off a Heineken. What if? Coincidence? A lead perhaps! He'd delay his visit with Mr. Nathan Bass until a call back from Detective Carl Swanson.

Nathan lay awake the next few nights. A pressure moved in around him. That Dan fella. Now some other insurance investigator asking around recently. Jeanie, a clerk at the town hall talked a bit too loud at the diner while he sat a table away. And my Jan-Marie!

Would it really have lasted? Time to focus on a plan. Everything must be perfect!

# Chapter Fifteen

The Mercedes sped along Route 128. Her engine humming a powerful aria echoing against a star filled sky.    He parked on the garage third tier. Took two spaces, distrustful of anyone pulling in.

The 'Boys Club II' was just around the block. Stopping outside a large glass storefront, he adjusted the bleach-blonde hair piece, undid another button of the light pink shirt exposing his chest, and hung the chain pendant around his neck. The white scarf was a nice touch he re-thought.  Turning, he lifted the leather jacket checking the form the tight pants held. The hard plastic cup helped the front. He'd certainly be noticed!

He handed the tall, gangly feminine talking door guy the cover charge.  Straightening himself so as to appear confident and a couple, "hi you", and stares told him he had come to the right place, and on the right night.

Two stools side by side were free at the bar. Room for a prospect he was thinking. He took a seat, ordering a gin and tonic, and spun around to check the floor. Size them up. He was 5'10". He weighed 167 lbs. He had an average frame. He had brown hair, hazel eyes, good teeth with no flaws. And so must be his selection.

Early on he spotted at least six closely fitting this category. Good! He didn't really want to have to return here so often as to make himself noticed. And didn't want the hassle of transforming himself over and over.

Best case!  Lure his likeness in tonight. A horny one looking for a 'one-nighter'.  A couple drinks, slip a pill, just enough to get him to the car.

His tongue slipped over his lips as he grinned in the direction of a likeness. Handsome looking dudes, he thought, sitting here feeling inside like the biggest fool.

Was that a smile back? Nathan's hand slid over his chest playing with the gold pendant. Then moved to pat the stool next to him.

As pretty boy came closer, Nathan's eyes caught the leather-covered bulge in leather pants, hard nipples under a sheer silk tight white tee. He tempered the urge to laugh, instead standing and nonchalantly running one hand through his blonde tresses.

Nathan's hand out-stretched. "Hi my cool looking friend. I'm Nate. Join me," not asking, but directing.

"Hi there yourself. " I'm Gregory. Love too."

Ignoring the idea of his moving too fast, Nathan momentarily ogled Gregory's lap. I'm really digging your leather Gregory."

"You're a fast mover there, Nate."

Nathan took a long moment to gulp a mouthful of gin and swallow. Not responding to the question, he stared into Gregory's eyes.

Lowering his glass, Gregory continued. "No long term relationship I take it? Or out for a quickie because of one?"

Nathan countered. "You don't want to rush what could work out to be something special. Do you?"

Gregory shifted on his stool, his knee sliding in rubbing against Nathan.

The thought crossed Nathan's mind. The embarrassment he endured at the adult video store was paying off. He had studied those two films concentrating several times on one, 'Gay Men Encounters.' It displayed more of the body language, conversation, and more on sexual moves. Which he would require later. He now recalled a couple pages on the trait of many gay men. Jealousy! He wanted to test it out. But would it lure his new partner in, or discourage the mood?

He tried but couldn't avoid a grin at this thought. Gregory's eyes widened. "What is that grin about? Nathan decided to build on this in his little game. "Nothing I suppose. But that big hunk of a black dude over there is flirting. And he can surely see we have a thing going."

Gregory instantly turned on his stool. He couldn't miss the beauty in the muscle shirt. Thick toned biceps and shoulder muscle, six pack rippling as he danced. Thick thighs and a real package bulging in between.

"He's nobody!" Gregory quickly scoffed. He's in here three maybe four times a week.

Thinks he's something. Talk is he's married with kids. Comes here to play his side game. Likes man-lips on his cock. The wife must not like it. Or doesn't have the", pausing to place his hand on Nathan's thigh. "You know. The know-how." His hand moved up, one finger tapping on just the right spot.

Nathan felt himself warming, a few beads of sweat on his forehead. He was not aroused. Just feeling suddenly anxious about this whole thing. He emptied his glass, asking for a refill. He had to keep control. Would Gregory question his non-arousal? He went from one finger to two placed around the head of his dick.

Nathan thought of Jan-Marie laying naked, arms outstretched, smiling, beckoning him teasingly by touching herself, her nipples, her shaved little pussy. His eyes closed now.

"Well that's more to my liking," Gregory's hand now surrounding the full package "Nice big balls too! More to play with! Take a look at me big Nate."

Nathan looked over and down. Somehow gay Gregory had slipped his pecker out. His hand moved slowly up and down. "You had me juicing in my pants, sweet Nate. Got to put it away though before I get caught. You can sneak a feel, but management frowns on public display. And you never know when an undercover is visiting. "You've really got me hot sweet guy."

Nathan downed his drink. " I think we both know, sweet man, that this meeting wasn't meant for long conversation over drinks and dinner. Why don't we get out of here and really enjoy each other in this moment?" His hand reached Gregory's crotch. "Oh yeah, baby, I want you to put this in all the right places." He stood rubbing his against Gregory's knee and placed a lasting firm kiss on his lips. Doing so, his mind was racing. This had better work!

Gregory slipped off his stool, " Even if you're leading me on Sweet Nate, lead on. Lead on" He repeated this several more times aloud brushing through the throng and out to the street.

Nathan motioned, "I'm parked in the garage around the corner."

My car there as well," Gregory countered, his arm sliding around Nathan's lower back. "Your car or mine?"

"You like to wear leather. My interior is leather, comfy soft, and heated. Or we could drive somewhere more in keeping with the mood. Enjoy some wine, lit candles, incense burning, soft music. And sheets are satin."

Nathan paused, stopped walking. His left hand reached the back of Gregory's head, his right hand nestled at his crotch. This, he hoped would seal this deal. As he pulled Gregory down planting a long kiss, his tongue slipped inside. He could feel the instant response in his right hand as he squeezed gently.

"I live only forty-minutes down the highway. I'll bring you back to your car in the morning. You've already paid to park the night. We'll come back here for a nice brunch at Miles Place on Newbury Street. Gregory rested his head against Nathan. "You have everything thought out. Sounds wonderful to me! Satin sheets! Get this Mercedes ripping will you?"

Nathan was toying now. "Did I mention the outside hot tub?"

Sensual 'Oohs!' Exiting Gregory's throat. "I'm going to stay hard for this ride. You too!" Hand cupping Nathan's lap. Nathan stepped on the gas. He glanced, grinning into the rear view mirror.

Nathan walked slowly from cage to cage stopping at three holding yellow Labs. Returning to the first he asked to see her up close. The attendant complied, willfully telling of her fine traits. Nathan did the same exam of two others. The third had the most similar mass and bone structure to his Lady.

After providing a handsome financial donation to the handler of the shelter, he loaded her into the truck.

Pulling a safe distance away, he removed the blonde "gay" wig. Although he thought there no reason, however should the unspeakable occur, he pictured the attendant not able to recall any one of his true images having visited. The yellow Lab was taken by a guy with blonde hair. Named Mr. Lambert from Plymouth.

I came to know Mr. Lambert who lived on Main Street in Plymouth from the obituary posted in last week's Enterprise. Think it all out precisely. The predictable. The incalculable.

I'll get towels from the warmer near the hot tub. They take the chill off on the way outside. You can make yourself comfortable in the den.

See the bar? Open that bottle of Chablis on the counter." "Be happy too!" Obvious excitement in Gregory's voice.

Nathan detoured to the car retrieving the small bottle from the compartment. Then headed to grab the towels. Gregory met him as he came through the French doors holding out the glass of wine.

"Thank you Gregory." He held up the towels. "Nothing like a warm towel nestled around you on the way to the tub."

In an instant it seemed, Gregory had stripped down to a purple thong. Though with his excited anticipation, no thong could contain him as it held against his inner thigh.

"Come on, a big boy. Let's not keep the warm tub waiting " And out the doors he scooted. Nathan chuckled now. More relaxed that his work nearly done. But remaining edgy enough to carefully carry through. Imagine a guy scooting to a hot tub naked in lift heeled shoes?

While Gregory slid under the water, Nathan slipped two small pills into his glass. Feeling very uncomfortable with this man holding him, working his dick and about to go further, he pulled his head from the water. "Take a breath sweet guy. I want this to last. I love foreplay. The build-up of momentum. You know!"

"I know. But this thing," grasping hard and pointing at Nathan, " is about ready to explode. I'd rather it not just wasted into thin air. I want it someplace warm. And I know you would too."

"Let's drink some wine first. Enjoy this time." Nathan handed him the glass.

"You're right of course, big Nate." Gregory emptied his full glass in one long drink. Nate smiled.

" That a boy! Come sit close. Make your free hand useful. Kiss me you gorgeous man."

Gregory came forward kneeling in the water, his lips covering Nathan's chest and stomach. Gregory's head fell heavy underwater. Nathan stood up. "Sweet dreams love."

"I'll fetch you shortly", he spoke into the night. The storage freezer would contain Gregory and his Lab companion until the time right.

The Lady was wired. She smelled the other dog from the moment of arrival. But no more. Even so she sniffed and roamed every inch of the yard.

# Chapter Sixteen

Sweet Jan-Marie figured something up. My absence on two nights to Boston, the pound, an overnight to Pennsylvania.

Jan-Marie was trembling. She stammered nervously. "What are you doing? Where are you taking me? Why the blindfold?"

"Hush my darling-sweetheart," his hand brushing her shoulder as he drove. "Nothing to fear. I am done here. I don't want to go on. I thought of taking you with me. But, I cannot come to grips of harming you as in the past. I care too much. I found love with you."

Her mind was whirling! What does he speak of? Is this to be my end? His tone projecting sincerity being the voice of that Demon within? The one she formally acquainted with? She decided not to question. Though remain vigilant.

He had come across this vacated run-down cottage during his search weeks ago. He had revisited it twice finding no evidence that it occupied or even visited. He had taken life, and now, because of letting his guard down, became weak. He was going to give life. He knew now that he must not mistakenly allow feelings of fondness, of passion, to sneak in again. He would find no other like her. After all he'd put her through. What she had endured. For him! He knew he could not rid himself of the selfish madness imprisoned within. Deep down realizing that he enjoyed it. He must leave all this behind.

The movie reel in Nathan's mind rewound. The beginning. That first time. The trial-run, two and a half years earlier. It was near, but hardly perfection. Nearly, not acceptable. The timing, the passion, the clean-up, not in sync. He had to be in total control. The combination of a struggle, and seeing his victim in a pose. The feeling of his condemnation, followed by the self-embodied act of ultimate pleasure consummating to a swift ending, not yet achieved.

She hot at first, perspiring, before becoming rigid, like a frozen cadaver laying limp. And whimpering. He had acted hastily. Not the rave performance intended. A small town girl, no make-up, un-shampooed hair, crotch-odor. Her life in a shambles. She would not be missed.

It was a dive. Hanging clouds of smoke circled the ceiling, choking your throat. An old juke box sang 'Crazy'. The bartender, a real joker, pouring and sharing shots with the regulars.

The cab driver told Nathan it wasn't a bad place, just a bit old. Good pulled-pork sandwiches, and the drinks reasonable. And, yes, a girl or two hung there for the right stranger.

Jimbo, the bartender called her Holly. Her eyes followed the waitress to my corner table. She saw my look. She turned back to the bar shifting on the stool just enough, sharing her thong and butterfly tattoo.

It didn't take long after exchanging looks in the bar mirror, that she swivelled on her stool. Crossing one long lean leg over the other, she lifted her beer, the tip of her tongue playing with the heady foam before sliding it to her mouth, smiling again.

I pulled out the empty chair from my table, and smiled back. She bent, adjusting the high heeled shoe she had been swinging on her toes like a see-saw. The short mini-skirt slid up each thigh as her legs spread to slide from the bar stool. The brief show of her crotch told she liked pink lace.

She was ripe for picking. But he had to find out if she a favorable candidate? Who is she? Divorced, no kids, living alone?

Within fifteen minutes he knew. Divorced, no kids, and in her own apartment. Lives and works in the next town over. A forty minute drive, but she feels at home and comfortable here in Lou's Place.      Ripe for the picking?

Holly, I admit, almost too much to handle. This girl was sensuous, passionate, and did it all, no asking? When my madness surfaced, she fought. I knew she would. She scratched and clawed my coveralls until coming under control.

Terror grew in her eyes. The sex the ultimate exhilaration before the act culminating as she squirmed and whined like a cornered cat. Eye shadow running mixing with blood splatter on cheap make-up.

I still wonder, now and again, if she ever was found?

Bags packed, I smiled into the mirror. Let's go home!

He was pulling down the narrow dirt road, suddenly not understanding how he arrived. As if he had driven through another time.

He parked at the cottage. Once inside, he released Jan-Marie's bindings, asking her to sit at the table as he filled the tea kettle and placed it on the stove. He set his chair close beside her.

"My sweet girl." His eyes washed over hr face. "Jan-Marie, I must let you go. Things have changed. Ii will miss you. I ask nothing more of you. I wish you and Mama had met. She would have liked you. He paused, standing to lift the kettle. He poured over tea bags in each cup.

Jan-Marie's hands trembled as she lifted her cup. Her lips shook her words, "What is your plan for me?" Tears filled her eyes, her cup banged on the saucer. Her hands cupped her face.

"I want to know," squeaked from her throat.

He took her hands in his. This has to end. As these words locked in her ears, as did the dizziness, and a final prayer for her soul.

Janine would find the cell phone beside her in several hours, once awake from her pill driven nap.

Even the thought of a final romantic-sexual experience eluding his mind. He combed her hair, applied make-up, dressed her in that black dress, and left her on the couch.

He kissed her lips without passion. "Even though I must try, I shall never forget you. Have no fear. I am moving to a better place."

He sped away, tossing the directions out the window, erasing landmarks from his mind. Forget this place! Do not turn around!

# Chapter Seventeen

Sirens wailed! Emergency vehicles raising dust clouds through which flames could be seen catching lower Pine limbs bent over the cabin. A hunter had reported it by cell phone.

The structure was engulfed when apparatus pulled up. Twenty-five mph wind gusts made quick work of it. Firefighters, therefore, concentrating on flames spreading further into the forest.

According to the news, officials recovered the body of the owner, and his dog. Early investigation determined the source starting at a faulty outlet connection at the hot tub on the rear deck. A location where the first flames and smoke would have gone unnoticed. And furthest away from the bedroom  where pieces of a smoke detector was found screwed to the underside of a ceiling joist, a corroded battery inside. But had it worked? Theorized, now that heavy smoke overcame sleeping victims.

Chief Broderick read the headline in the Local section of the newspaper the next morning. The name Bass jumped out at him. He called Dan who confirmed that the same area he had visited. They were on there way twenty minutes later.

They spoke constantly on the way down route 44, interjecting and surmising.  Joe was beside himself, and bitter. "This is no coincidence, Dan. The families farm. Now this!"

"Come-on Joe. There was no evidence on this guy. No grounds. Only speculation, like you are doing now. We'll visit the scene, talk to the police chief and the Fire Marshall.

A call to the Plymouth police advised that the Chief, Fire Chief, and Fire Marshall were back on  the fire scene this morning.

Dan and Joe leaned against the Fire Chief's SUV while he updated them on findings.

"All pretty cut and dry," said Fire Chief Swanson.

"Guy hunting pheasants saw the flames. Said it was going good even then. Was engulfed when we got here? One tanker truck doused what remained of the structure. The other tanker had to concentrate on containing the surrounding Pines and brush. That hunter hadn't seen it we'd be fighting a forest fire."

Dan spoke up. "Chief ? I was here with the owner some months ago. The time we were investigating the murders. I see the scorched pick-up truck there. This Bass fellow also drove a Mercedes. His pride and joy, as he himself had mentioned."

"Don't know anything of that, Dan. Maybe sold it? Was his guy a suspect back then?"

Joe cleared his throat. "Well, yes and no. We learned of unconfirmed information that he possibly carried a bitterness over the family homestead, the farm that is, having been sold from under him, so to speak. He had lived somewhere out of state we believe, but still held ownership of the house and a few acres his father has provided him. His father had married a younger woman.

She sold real estate. Mr. Bass passed away. His widow moved to Florida. Dan here was building a profile of the murderer. Some traits of Nathan Bass were a consideration in that profile. Added to all this is the home where he lived burned to the ground. No evidence of arson. A specific source, undetermined. Surmised, and with conditions of teens there, partying on the property, started it. You can see now why we're here."

Dan asked the Chief if he minded his borrowing his boots to check around the debris. "Not at all, Dan. But there isn't much left. State Fire Marshall over there and two of my men raked through most of it."

Dan scuffled about wet soot, kicking over charred two-by-sixes and two-by-fours. After half an hour pulled the boots off. The small shed was heavily charred but standing. Dan walked in the open doors.

It was empty. Dusty old shelves. A couple large pieces of plywood strung across the rafters for storage above. Standing on an old wooden milk box he stretched his head reaching only inches above. Nothing there. As he reached one hand to steady himself on the crate one section of plywood moved. A section of crumpled newspaper fell to the floor. Seeing nothing else he jumped down. The piece of newspaper stuck to the heel of his shoe. He stepped on it with his other shoe, lifting. Still stuck, he reached down. His eyes reacted wide. There on that wrinkled page was a headline. 'Open-House Killer Strikes Again'.

Dan carefully unfolded a second page. A partial page of the Real Estate section.

"Holy shit!" He ran out. "Holy shit, again. Joe! Look at this!" He handed it to Joe, pointing where someone had circled open house locations.

Joe fell back against the car. "My god! Dan! What the fuck! Who would do this, save this, if not? .

"Geezus! We had him right here. I really fucked up Dan!"

Dan understood Joe's reaction, also a noticeable stuttering before every second word. Beads of sweat lining his forehead, and his breathing, heavier between words.

"Joe, for god-sakes. Stop this bullshit right now. I and a lot of other people were with you on this. We all fucked up. Then again this Bass was really clever. Now he's dead. Let it go. He got what he deserved!" Joe leaned back resting against his cruiser. Dan looked away a moment, feeling just as guilty, if not more so. He the expert?

The autopsy of what remained of the body turned up nothing suspicious. The bracelet on the charred left wrist bone engraved NATHAN. Teeth had no fillings. No cause for forensics. The dog proved to be a Lab. Metal tag on the collar, 'LADY'.

With no conclusive findings, the summation by all was that Nathan Bates, their possible killer at large. And that he, deservedly so, had been consumed in his own hellish inferno.

Joe Montane spoke with the Chief for the final time by telephone. He would await the report from the Chief, combine it into his final summation before forwarding to CMS Insurance.

Nathan missed his Mercedes. There are others. He would have one once in his new place. He felt assured the guy he sold it to would care for it as he had. There was no way he could have left it to burn.

Planning to steal it back before heading out of town he had a key made before the sale. The thought of getting out of town unnoticed, though changed his mind.

Would be a pretty stupid move! A burned-up corpse being pulled over for car theft. Where would his glorious future be then?

His Maries' not making his acquaintance? That would be shameful.

# Chapter Eighteen

The ambulance driver caught a glimpse of her sitting on the large rock at the entrance of a dirt road. Her black dress imaging her silhouette against the skyline and ocean.

Her story unfolded. Unraveling each gory detail page by page into her book of horror. It would likely be a continuing nightmare for Janine to bear for a long, long time.

She had remembered just as her mind was blurring, part of what he said. She revealed this to Joe. 'That he was going to a better place.'

Did it mean he faulted the outlet? Was the fire accidental, or intentional?. No one would know. And it seemed after a time, no one cared.

This seemed especially so to Joe, who could no longer fight the demon holding him. He took retirement from the force two months later. Content now working three nights a week in security, and spending valuable time with family.

Town Selectmen, finding no current officer vying for the Chief position, posted it for outside candidates. All figured Detective Paulson would go for it, but he had opted for a position with the State Police.

Dan married Jen. They added on a study and second bath room. And, he sold his half of the business to his partner. Time to settle he realized.

The sign on his desk. CHIEF DAN HUDSON

"Nathan took the Motel office keys from the previous owner. "Good luck Nate. Somehow I don't remember your name as Nate? Then again, don't recall any other either?"

Nathan smiled. " I'm awful with names myself."

" The old man lit his cigarette.  Oh well. Getting old, I suppose. Anyway, never thought I'd see you back our way. Never mind your taking me up on that old offer."

Patting Lady. "Well sir, I like small rural towns. And this may turn out as a sound investment.  You see, as I understand it, Real Estate is really taking off around here."


ENDING . . . [ ? ]

# Dedication

This not the favored genre that my sister, Shirley, might select for her reading enjoyment.   However, she would have read, and critiqued it for me willingly.  And, not have held back.

   Though out of love for her brother, she would, as her practice, voiced encouragement either way.

   It is in loving memory, Shirl, [one of four wonderful sisters], that I dedicate this endeavor.


   Your loving Brother,

                                                              Fran  02/2009